Jackie Womack

"Don't Run From Me!

I know when a woman wants me to kiss her, and you wanted it, Tally—you wanted it as much as I did, so where does that leave all your fine theories about love and happily ever after?"

"I don't want to talk abou

"No, I'll bet you don
tone changed. Lifting
softly on her nape. "B
or not you're honest en

Her voice hoarse with e rrassment, she turned and shook his hand from her arm. "All right, so I admit you're expert enough to make a woman want you—at least temporarily; but it's only a—only a chemical reaction!"

DIXIE BROWNING,
a native of North Carolina, many of her stories are born as she travels from her home in Winston-Salem to her cottage in Frisco on Hatteras Island. "I have taken characters' names from the mailboxes along my route." She confided. She is also an accomplished watercolor artist, as well as a writer.

Dear Reader:

Silhouette has always tried to give you exactly what you want. When you asked for increased realism, deeper characterization and greater length, we brought you Silhouette Special Editions. When you asked for increased sensuality, we brought you Silhouette Desire. Now you ask for books with the length and depth of Special Editions, the sensuality of Desire, but with something else besides, something that no one else offers. Now we bring you SILHOUETTE INTIMATE MOMENTS, true romance novels, longer than the usual, with all the depth that length requires. More sensuous than the usual, with characters whose maturity matches that sensuality. Books with the ingredient no one else has tapped: excitement.

There is an electricity between two people in love that makes everything they do magic, larger than life—and this is what we bring you in SILHOUETTE INTIMATE MOMENTS. Look for them this May, wherever you buy books.

These books are for the woman who wants more than she has ever had before. These books are for you. As always, we look forward to your comments and suggestions. You can write to me at the address below:

Karen Solem
Editor-in-Chief
Silhouette Books
P.O. Box 769
New York, N.Y. 10019

DIXIE BROWNING

Practical Dreamer

Published by Silhouette Books New York
America's Publisher of Contemporary Romance

SILHOUETTE BOOKS, a Simon & Schuster Division of
GULF & WESTERN CORPORATION
1230 Avenue of the Americas, New York, N.Y. 10020

Distributed by Pocket Books

ISBN: 0-671-57221-0

First Silhouette Books printing May, 1983

10 9 8 7 6 5 4 3 2 1

Map by Ray Lundgren

America's Publisher of Contemporary Romance

Printed in the U.S.A.

Other Silhouette Books by Dixie Browning

Unreasonable Summer
Tumbled Wall
Chance Tomorrow
Wren of Paradise
East of Today
Winter Blossom
Renegade Player
Island on the Hill
Logic of the Heart
Finders Keepers
Loving Rescue
A Secret Valentine

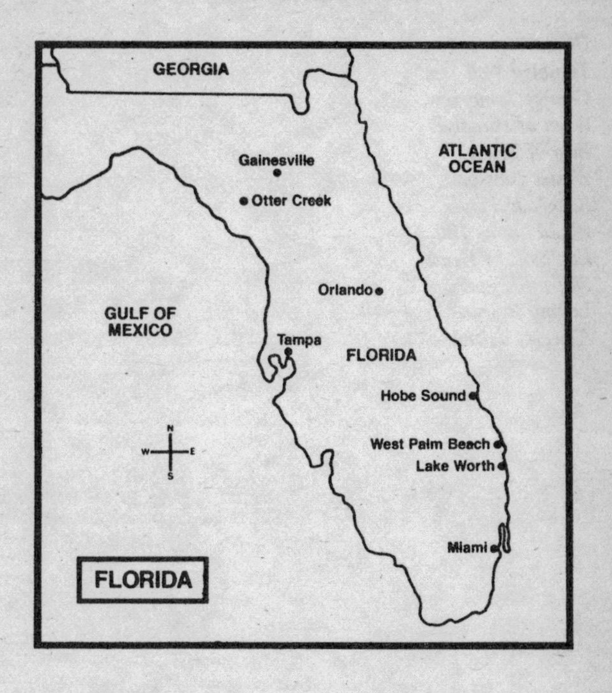
GEORGIA
ATLANTIC
OCEAN
Gainesville
Otter Creek
Orlando
GULF OF
MEXICO
Tampa
FLORIDA
Hobe Sound
N
W
E
S
West Palm Beach
Lake Worth
Miami
FLORIDA

Chapter One

"And whose little wifey will you be today?" Tally Fitzsimmons muttered to her mirror image as she yanked a loose thread from the buttonhole of her periwinkle blue shirtwaist. The style might be timeless, but the workmanship certainly wasn't. Still, after three and a half years of hard service, she shouldn't complain.

Hopping on one foot, she tugged at the heel strap of her sling-backed pump and promised herself to steal a few hours next week to work on a tan. It was ridiculous to live in Florida year round and still be as pale as a gooseberry!

As usual, she walked to work. With Claire and Judy on vacation in Las Vegas and both cars in the carport, she could have driven, but there was no point in cultivating expensive habits. Besides, she enjoyed the walk along Flagler. The six blocks to

Clematis Street took her past the municipal yacht club, and on a day like this, with the wind ruffling the surface of Lake Worth, the water looked almost purple.

Her step took on an added spring and a slight smile touched her normally grave features. With her stepmother and her stepsister away, it was a vacation for her, as well. Only one bed to make, one breakfast to get, and her own things to wash out before she left for work.

Turning right on Clematis, she quickened her step, inhaling a breeze laden with flower fragrance, salt air, exhaust fumes, and someone's burning bacon. She felt the usual surge of expectancy. It happened whenever she came off a long-term assignment and reported to Sara for her next one. Nine times out of ten it would be more of the same—rescuing some poor man whose wife was due back after an extended trip by hiring and supervising a corps of cleaners for an hour or two and personally taking care of all the loose ends, or playing surrogate mama to a flock of children while the real thing took a few days off for a quiet nervous breakdown.

There were housemaids and baby-sitters readily available, and for considerably less, but anyone who was willing to pay the hefty rates at HouseSpouse, Inc. was guaranteed a capable, executive-type jack-of-all-trades, who could delegate as needed or run the show single-handed. Tally was quite accustomed to shopping for children's school wardrobes and sewing in dozens of name tags herself. She could select a gift to fit both any occasion and any pocketbook, could plan a formal dinner and personally supervise everything from invitations to flowers to securing extra staff, and bright and early the next day, she could herd a covey of cub scouts to and from a cookout and still find a moment to get an estimate on a crumpled fender and make an appointment to have junior's braces adjusted.

The contract HouseSpouse, Inc. insisted all their clients sign spelled out the parameters of the duties that could normally be expected, and they did not include heavy housework. Accustomed to taking over in the middle of a domestic crisis, when all rules flew out the window, Tally could judge to a hair when and where to draw the line. Even the loftiest chairman of the board occasionally had to pour his own coffee, but Tally also wasn't above pitching in in an emergency.

Not that she'd ever have to worry about being an office fetch-it—or an office anything else. By the time it became obvious that there wouldn't be any funds for her to go on to college, her only skills revolved around the housework she had done ever since her father had remarried. It was not her chosen role in life, by any means, but when it became obvious that Rex Fitzsimmons had deserted his family, which included a wife, a daughter and a stepdaughter, she had pitched in willingly to assuage her guilty conscience. Claire had been under no obligation to give her a home. Her stepmother worked hard at her own career and was just beginning to get ahead, but it was expensive to maintain a house and support a teenaged daughter of her own. It was only fair that Tally take over the chores and chip in from her meager earnings at the day-care center, where she had worked every vacation.

When Judy had gone off to the University of Miami there was less to do at home, and Tally had been fortunate enough to land a job with House-

Spouse. The commission was respectable, and the work, while seldom very glamorous, was varied enough to be interesting.

On her way to the elevators, Tally lifted a hand in reply to a smile from one of the barbers. The old office building housed a variety of enterprises, and Tally enjoyed the casual contacts. She stepped off the elevator and hurried to Sara Drummond's office, bypassing the handkerchief-sized waiting room. Sara was on the phone, and Tally allowed her gaze to be drawn by the sliver of sky and rooftops visible through the office's single window. For just an instant, a swift surge of longing arose in her, and then she put it down just as swiftly. Nine A.M. was no time to indulge herself in a bout of foolish daydreaming.

"Yes, I understand, Mr. Coulter. That's right, we've done your dinners before . . . yes, that was Sybil. She's not available just now, but I'm sure . . . yes, we can do that. All right, then, I'll send someone out this morning. Young and fetching, right, Mr. Coulter! Bye now." Sara grimaced at Tally and hung up the phone. "I wouldn't take that stipulation from just any man, but old Mr. C.'s a doll. Rich as Croesus, but lonely. Poor old soul, he'll talk the ears off a brass monkey, but he's harmless—I have Sybil's word on it. She's done a few dinners for him, and I think he just wants someone to pay him a bit of attention—someone besides his family, that is."

Sara pushed her colorfully framed glasses back up her nose and frowned momentarily before crossing to the filing cabinet. "C . . . Colvin, Cotter . . . Coulter." She removed a folder, dropped into her swivel chair and crossed one white-clad leg over the other. Sara always wore white, claiming it spared her making the decision of what to wear, but she varied the effect by sporting a different pair of glasses for each day of the week—each more flamboyant than the last.

"Oh, yes—it's Addie time again."

Tally waited. Sara would get around to explaining as soon as she had scanned the contract copies and accompanying notes.

"Okay, no problem—get Flores to cater this one. Mr. Coulter doesn't want to impress anyone but his sister Addie—and not for the usual reasons, either. Once a year she makes a pilgrimage, hoping to catch her brother in dire straits so she can yank him back up to her home and make his last days pure hell. You know the type. All you have to do is make it look as if the old fellows—there are two of them, by the way, uncle and nephew—are thriving and surrounded by friends. He likes young people—especially," the older woman added with a grin, "young women. Fancies himself a latter-day John Travolta, according to Sybil, so humor him a bit. He's a good customer."

"Sounds thrilling," Tally said dryly. Actually, after spending two weeks living with the three inexhaustible Markerson girls while their parents were on a business trip to Kowloon, a couple of senior swingers would be welcome relief.

"You're due a plum after the Markerson deal. I understand those girls are a handful."

"For an octupus! I can't believe I was ever that bad!" Tally picked another thread from another buttonhole.

Sara smiled over her glasses. "Next time I'll send Kelsey—she'll jerk a knot in 'em. Anyhow, I promise you the very next plum that falls off the tree, no matter who else is available."

"Just make sure it's not another green persimmon. When is this dinner supposed to take place? It's not an overnight job, is it?" Tally didn't like to leave the house empty at night. The neighborhood was still basically sound, but a few blocks over blight had set in pretty badly.

"The dragon's due in tomorrow, I think, so you'd better trot on out there. It's north of town." Sara slid a contract form across the desk. "Here's the address. Take a cab and charge it to expenses."

The Coulter men, Hiram and Francis, captured her heart from the very first. Francis, the younger of the pair, seldom opened his mouth to say a word that didn't have to do with the succulents he grew in every available sunny window. The sometimes lovely, sometimes grotesque cacti thrived under his paternal care, and they, plus the nightly game of mah jong, were seemingly his only interests in life.

Hiram, at eighty-one, still managed a rheumy sparkle of enthusiasm as the dour housekeeper, Mrs. Stoner, showed Tally into a room that could only be called a parlor. Dressed in sharply creased white flannels, with an ascot tucked into the neck of his pink shirt and a navy blazer complete with tarnished club ensignia, he apologized for his slowness in rising as she entered the room.

"It's the humidity, you know," he explained. "Creeps into a man's bones when he gets to be sixty . . . well, seventy," he amended ruefully, and then, with a singularly sweet smile, he sighed. "Perhaps I meant eighty."

Between conferring with the housekeeper, with Flores, the caterer, and Hiram Coulter, Tally found herself the recipient of more Coulter confidences than she really cared to share. It was obvious that, living in the old mausoleum of a house with a taciturn housekeeper and a preoccupied nephew, the old man was terribly lonely. He followed her around like a spaniel, rambling about his sister and a great-nephew who he claimed was the very image of himself when he was a dashing young rogue.

She listened and smiled and added an occasional remark as she went about her duties. She also accepted the occasional pats on the shoulder or arm in the innocent way they were intended. If there was one thing she understood, it was loneliness—especially now that David, too, was half a world away.

"When the day comes that I look forward to Addie's visitation," Hiram confessed as Tally checked through the enormous linen supply for an unyellowed tablecloth, "then I know I'm in trouble. Terrible woman, my sister! Seventeen cats and still she won't be satisfied until she has me to manage, too. Comes here year after year, hoping to catch me in a weak moment and drag me up to Siler City with her, but she'll not catch me napping, no-siree bob! Not 's long as I can keep my wits about me."

Tally folded a handsome cutwork cloth over her arm and eyed a plump-sided coffee service on a dusty tea cart. There was enough silver around the house to plate a battleship, and all of it black with tarnish. "Well, it's your house and your life, and you don't look in need of a keeper to me," she assured her employer, pretending not to see the fine tremor in his hands.

"We won't tell Addie about your part in our little game, will we? The old girl thinks I've outlived all my friends, and the truth is I have, but let's give her a run for her money—managin' old battle-axe," he grumbled.

Tally was told to prepare for five and Hiram

insisted he wanted her to play hostess at the table. "We'll put Addie and Francis together—she can't rattle poor Francis—and Thane can take the other side."

Thane Coulter, it seemed, was the great-nephew, and according to Hiram, the self-righteous young man was far too busy making money hand over fist to do more than meddle now and then. "Thinks he has to save me from my sins," the old man muttered. "Thinks the world's full of pretty little gals just waitin' to dance a fandango with an old coot like me! I let him think it—does me a darned sight more good than all the pills and nostrums my doctor charges me a fortune for."

Sounds like a grand and glorious evening, Tally grimaced inwardly. These two old sweethearts deserved better than that from their only two relatives, and Tally was determined to prove that they had at least one able-bodied friend to look after their interests, even if their own flesh and blood couldn't spare the time to liven up their last years!

The following morning Tally arrived early, carrying her small overnight case containing her evening clothes and the last of the perfume her father had brought her from France years ago. It had probably turned by now. She had been saving it for a special occasion, but since David left there simply hadn't been any.

As she climbed the broad golden oak stairway, she marveled that it had only been a day ago that she had first set foot in the Coulter mansion. With the aid of Mrs. Stoner and a fleet of professional cleaners, they had polished every visible surface in the high-ceilinged rooms and placed enormous flower arrangements in strategic locations to direct a critical eye away from faded brocades and worn tapestries. But not even two big bowls of shasta daisies and acacia could do much to brighten Miss Addie's room, with the heavy old oak furniture and the dark, silk-covered walls.

Tally hung her dinner dress in the closet of the room she had chosen to change in. If there had been time, she'd have organized a team of gardeners to cut back some of the junglelike growth that threatened to envelop the house. Why couldn't the great-nephew look after that sort of thing? Was he blind to everything except his own selfish interests? If he had a shred of human decency . . .

But that wasn't her concern. It didn't pay to get involved in her clients' personal affairs. Still, in a remarkably short time, she had grown attached to those two aging darlings, and if she could prevent it, neither the dragon of a sister nor the hawk of a great-nephew was going to pry Hiram out of his home and stash him somewhere to wither away! Let the sister go back home and manage her seventeen cats. And as for the other one, he was probably just rubbing his palms together, waiting to get his hands on this property so he could rezone it and sell it for a fortune to some soulless conglomerate who would destroy it down to the last stained-glass window and golden oak pediment!

Tally was delegated to pick up Addie Coulter from Palm Beach International. She drove Hiram's vintage Cadillac, feeling as if she were handling a float in a parade, and was amused when she spotted the old woman immediately. The physical description helped—those solid dark eyebrows that contrasted with the white hair were identical to Hiram's—but it was her strident walk and her way of speaking that was the dead giveaway. With all the tact and finesse of a drill sergeant, she was telling a hapless young mother precisely what was wrong with her whining offspring and what to do about it. Addie Coulter, ferocious eyebrows, no-nonsense felt hat and all, was exactly as Tally had pictured her.

By the time Tally escaped to change for dinner, she was reasonably certain that nothing could go wrong with the carefully planned evening. The menu was simple and designed to seem as if it had been prepared in Mrs. Stoner's kitchen. Flores excelled at that sort of thing. She couldn't bring herself to lie about it if she were asked point-blank, but she hoped the overall impression was one of a well-run home. All she had to do was convince Miss Addie that the two Coulter men were nowhere near ready to be put out to pasture, thank you; and as for the greedy great-nephew, he'd probably be too busy taking inventory of the silver to wonder who had produced the standing rib roast and the green beans almondine.

Brushing the thick black flyaway hair into a swirl on top of her head, she anchored it with half a dozen tortoiseshell pins and turned her head to admire the effect. Hiram would appreciate the Gibson Girl style, even though her dinner dress was strictly modern and extremely simple. She had only the one, a nicely cut sheath in an ice blue fabric that looked like silk, but wasn't. She had bought it on sale two years ago, and given the transient nature of her work, it served her well enough as an all-purpose formal. If she ever had to attend two social functions in the same household, she'd be out of luck. As for her evening sandals, the less said, the better! For the sake of her poor feet, they'd have to be replaced soon.

Fortunately, she didn't require much in the way of

makeup. She had inherited her father's "black Irish" coloring. They shared the same large, slightly near-sighted blue eyes embedded in a luxuriant growth of black lashes. Rex Fitzsimmons wore glasses, but Tally had ignored her increasingly abstract view. One of these days she'd treat herself to a pair of contacts, or perhaps a wardrobe of glamorous specs like Sara's, but for the time being, every cent she managed to save put her that much closer to Australia and David.

A frown flickered across her pale forehead as she touched the small Tiffany-set diamond on her left hand. No time to worry about David now. It was time to go downstairs and act as a buffer between Hiram and his self-seeking relatives. Sweet Francis didn't need a buffer. Little, if anything, disturbed his benign preoccupation with his plants.

Detouring by the kitchen to see that all was going according to schedule, she could hear Miss Addie's strident tones holding forth on the variety of diseases to be contracted in heathen places. She *did* pick cheerful topics for dinner conversation. Still, as long as her attention was on some other continent, maybe she wouldn't set her sights on Hiram. Tilting her head in a manner meant to indicate self-confidence, Tally entered the parlor.

She would have recognized him for a Coulter anywhere. It was the eyebrows again, although this time they surmounted eyes that could have been chipped from any glacier. Thane Coulter was dressed traditionally in black and white, making a dramatic contrast to his already dramatic coloring. His eyes followed her into the room as she crossed to Hiram's side, and she smiled up at the old man in as reassuring a manner as she could manage. She had sensed Thane Coulter's resentment as soon as she entered the room, and it only served to make her more determined than ever to bolster Hiram's position.

The introductions were made in Hiram's gallant and courtly manner. He introduced her to his grim-faced great-nephew as a "dear, kind young friend," and Tally watched appprehensively as he poured her a sherry, his trembling old hands spilling not a drop as he rattled decanter against glass. They smiled conspiratorially in relief, and then her eyes were drawn past the shoulder of Hiram's slightly dated dinner jacket to see Thane's glacial eyes probing her with open suspicion.

Good Lord, did he think she was going to abscond with the family jewels? Or was he afraid she'd lead his uncles astray with her womanly wiles?

They filed into the dining room and the glowering increased when Hiram seated Tally in the chair opposite him. Tally, hoping she wouldn't break out with a skin rash from such intense scrutiny, turned with spurious interest and asked Miss Addie if she planned to be in Florida long.

"Three days! 'S all I ever stay," retorted the indomitable woman. "I've told Hiram time and time again that a place that's got no seasons is unhealthy. Unnatural, if you ask me! Takes a good, hard winter to rid the system of all the pests that plague a mortal, and you can't tell me any different!"

Tally wouldn't dream of trying to tell her anything. She turned to Francis, but he was gazing abstractedly at a gloomy oil painting that depicted a young woman swinging under feather-duster trees, à la Fragonard. That left the other two Coulters. Attaching a determined smile on her face, she turned to Hiram and questioned him about the old bathhouse, gambling-club days on Palm Beach.

By the time the meal was over, Tally felt as if the smile had congealed on her face. The only consolation was that Miss Addie seemed to have enjoyed her meal. She had put away enough for two grown men, ignoring Tally's one or two forced conversational gambits. That had left Francis to dwell in his own private world, and Thane to glower, while Hiram regaled her with slightly risqué stories of his past—highly exaggerated, she suspected. Either that, or the days had held thirty-six hours back then, when he had gambled at Bradley's with some of the leading politicians of the time, had bought champagne at the Oasis for all of the Ziegfeld girls, and then worked off the effects at Gus's Baths before starting on the same round again.

And through it all, Tally grew increasingly aware that with his deep tan, his thick blond hair and those black brows over the chilling gray eyes, Thane Coulter was one of the most magnetically attractive men she had encountered in a long time. While she despised everything he stood for, she couldn't help but appreciate the inbred air of command that set him apart from every man she knew. He wore authority as if he were born to it, and the very sureness with which he moved set her nerves on edge. A woman would have to be a masochist to get involved with a man of that sort.

Of one thing she was certain: she was not going to stand by and watch him railroad his two uncles into a house full of cats just so he could build up his own estate on the ruins of theirs!

Back in the parlor, Tally sipped her demitasse and wriggled her toes in the miserable sandals. She was achingly tired. It seemed that she had been going flat-out ever since she had signed on at the agency, with weekends spent catching up on chores at home.

And hoarding every penny meant doing without a few conveniences—walking instead of driving, hand washing her good clothes instead of dry-cleaning them, and doing her own hair instead of patronizing a salon. She'd be less than honest if she didn't admit that sometimes she resented the money her stepsister seemed to have in endless supply for the small luxuries.

Through her befogged senses came the realization that Thane Coulter had been trying to get her attention. His impatient baritone rasp struck her ears unpleasantly as he asked if Miss Fitzsimmons would please excuse them for half an hour. "If you could bring yourself to do without my great-uncle's company, I'd like to speak to my relatives about a private matter." He stressed the word private, and Tally scrambled to her feet, furious for having been caught off guard. "I'm sure you wouldn't be interested in our private, family business, Miss Fitzsimmons, so if you don't mind . . . ?" Instead of his retiring with his relatives to the library, he was indicating that she should leave the room, like some school child in disgrace, and Tally hotly resented it.

"About time, too, Thane!" Miss Addie boomed. "What's this about getting involved with a bunch of foreigners? My father never had to go hat in hand to anybody, much less a bunch of heathens who don't even speak the King's English!"

Ignoring his great-aunt, Thane stood, legs braced apart as if he were on the bridge of a ship, and waited for Tally to collect herself and leave the room. By the time she reached the portiered arch she was scrambling with almost indecent haste.

"I'll see you before I leave, Hiram," she called out as a parting shot. At least that pair of vultures would know that she couldn't be intimidated so easily.

Hiram had at least one good friend who would stand by and see that he wasn't railroaded out of his very home!

Upstairs in the guest room, she dropped wearily down onto a striped satin slipper chair. How odd that she should feel such an affinity for two men she had never even heard of before yesterday—and such an antipathy to a third that she had never seen before tonight. Bushwhacked! That's what she was. The strain of worrying about her father, worrying about David, taking every assignment Sara handed her in order to build up her bank account—it was all beginning to tell on her. Fortunately she was as healthy as a horse, but even horses had to rest sometimes.

She slipped her feet out of the miserable silver sandals. Swollen feet and tight straps didn't mix very well. Leaning her head back against the cool satin, she allowed her lids to drift down over her tired eyes. She should have called a cab while she was in the kitchen. She had detoured by there to be sure the Flores people had cleared away sufficiently. With the last chore done, she could go home and collapse. Tomorrow, thank goodness, was Sunday, and she'd lie in bed until she darned well felt like getting up.

Random thoughts drifted through her mind: remember to get her white wedges repaired, and pick up Claire's cleaning before she got back from Vegas. Judy would be home for a few weeks, too, before she went back to Miami, and that thought brought with it a feeling of depression.

It was ironic, the way things had turned out. Rex Fitzsimmons had hoped to see his motherless daughter fit into a new family that included a new mother and a ready-made sister only a year and a half older, but somehow it had never worked out that way. Judy and Tally were totally different—nor could Claire ever take the place of Tally's own mother.

Nor, evidently, could she take the place of Rex's first wife. A sailor by profession, his visits home had dwindled to an occasional week and then to a few days every few months, and then he had stopped coming back altogether. As if by mutual agreement, none of the three women he had left behind mentioned his absence except obliquely. Claire's interest was taken up with her job, and Tally went about her chores silently, rationalizing that Rex had changed ships and was now doing much longer runs. Each day, though, her eyes went to the small pile of mail when she came home. Claire went through it first and then left the circulars and advertisements—and until six weeks ago, David's letters—for Tally to deal with.

David. How was it possible that the only three people in her life she had ever truly loved had disappeared from her life, one after another? Was it something to do with her? Did she lack some essential ingredient that rendered her unlovable? Did she suffer any of the dreadful afflictions so common in television commercials?

They had both been so excited when David had landed the overseas assignment with Allied so soon after graduation. He was extremely ambitious, and although it meant a painful separation for them, the pay was much higher than if he had gone to the New Jersey refinery. He had given Tally her engagement ring and she had depleted her savings to buy him a set of really good luggage. After that there had been a steady stream of letters, telling her about the apartment he shared with two other Allied geologists, of the opportunities for advancement, and how much he missed her and longed for the time when she could join him. They planned to be married as soon as he could swing a bungalow for the two of them.

But then his letters had slowed up—the vagaries of the postal system, she had thought at first. The occasional ones that reached her began to reflect a slight dissatisfaction, a restlessness, an impatience with the ponderous wheels of personal progress.

"The red tape would wrap around the globe twice and still be enough to trip a man up," he had written in his next to the last letter. "Just when I see a chance to move up a rung, someone jumps in ahead of me and shoves me against the wall. I'm telling you, honey, I can be a gentleman for just so long, and then David's going to start shoving, too! I'll make a place for myself with this outfit or move on to one that appreciates me."

It saddened her that he was no longer writing about making a place for *them*, but for *him*, and she told herself that it was only a figure of speech. But when the letters stopped coming and her last two were returned marked addressee unknown, she was more determined than ever to save every penny until she could pay her way out to Queensland. She knew David's pride. He didn't want to send for her until he had a home for them both, but she'd show him that she could work in Australia as well as he could. Together, they'd make it, even if the going was rough for the first few years.

Wearily, she opened her eyes and stretched. Time to make a move if she was going to get home tonight. She almost wished she could fall into bed right here, but with that eagle-eyed great-nephew in the house, she didn't dare. He'd probably be waiting at the door to check her purse and pockets before she left the premises!

One of her darned shoes had rolled under the bed, and jabbing about with her foot for it only pushed it farther under. Hitching up her long skirt against Mrs. Stoner's haphazard cleaning, Tally knelt and poked her head under the dust ruffle. "Darn," she grumbled as she peered about in the musty gloom and stretched to reach a palely gleaming silver strap.

Behind her the sound of a door opening and closing brought her startled head into contact with the bed rail. Rear end in the air and face burning, she backed out from under the heavy brocaded draperies, destroying her flattering Gibson Girl hairstyle in the process. What now?

Rising swiftly, she swayed on her feet, the sandal clutched tightly to her middle, and stared in dismay at the intimidating figure leaning against the closed door. His derisive scrutiny missed nothing of her dishevelment. She had a swift idea that he knew to a penny what she had paid for every stitch she had on, and when his scathing glance moved to the well-worn sandal, with its paper-thin, twice-repaired soles, she bristled defensively.

"Did you want me for something?" She tried for hauteur, but under the circumstances, it wasn't easy.

"Hardly!" The meaning was unmistakable. "How long have you known my uncles?"

The opening guns. Her head tilted back another two degrees. "Not terribly long, but then I don't measure friendship by the yardstick of time."

Moving past her, his glance took in her overnight case. A colorful fabric, it was bright and cheerful and hopelessly cheap looking against the splendid old brocade bedspread. The gaze moved back to her dress, her hair, and the silver sandal she clutched as if it were a shield. He added it all up, noted the total, and asked disparagingly, "All right, how much?"

Under the pitiless glare of the overhead fixture, Tally blinked. Was he asking her how much she was being paid for her services? Had Hiram buckled under his relentless tactics?

"How much?" he barked again.

Tally was tired. She had done nothing to rate his contempt—nothing except to try and make up to his poor uncle for the neglect by his own family! But as tired as she was, she was darned well not going to let poor Hiram down. He was stuck with his rotten family, but maybe a good friend would help make up for their callousness!

"Enough to make it worth my while," she snapped at him. It was no lie—and he could interpret it any way he pleased!

"There's a name for your kind of leech, you know." His eyes were expressionless as they roved over her unnaturally pale features, her large, shadowed eyes, but the curl of his mouth was unmistakable.

She had been on the verge of relenting and telling him exactly what she was doing here, but after that, she'd walk on hot coals before she'd justify her position in the Coulter household. Let him think the worst! Maybe it would give him a few bad moments between foreclosing mortages and hounding poor widows and orphans!

"Precisely how much more are you expecting to get out of my uncle in exchange for your . . . friendship?"

Oh, what she wouldn't give to be able to wipe that hateful sneer off his hard mouth! "I don't think it concerns you, Mr. Coulter. Hiram is old enough to look after himself."

Her peripheral vision took in the curl of his fists alongside those powerful, black-clad thighs, but her eyes were pinned to his peculiarly clear gray eyes. She could almost read his calculating mind, and the picture she felt he had of her was hardly flattering: too thin, too pale, cheaply dressed through either a lack of money or a lack of taste—or both.

Oh, no, he didn't bother to hide his unflattering opinion of her. Bracing the six feet some odd inches of granite clad in custom-tailored dinner suit, he put his proposition to her with no attempt to make it more palatable. "Look, Miss . . . I have neither the time nor the inclination to hang around and wet-nurse my uncle through his second childhood, so spit it out. How much will you take to clear out and let him off the hook? And don't go overboard! I could make it a case for the law, you know."

Tally was livid! She had run into a few sticky situations when someone mistook HouseSpouse for an escort service or a matrimonial bureau, but there had never been anything like this! Her temper backed her further into a corner. "You couldn't pay me enough, Mr. . . ." Purposely, she dropped his name in retaliation for the slurring way he had ignored hers.

"Don't overestimate your worth, girl, and don't push your luck. Just because a lonesome old man allows you to dress up and play lady of the manor, don't think you're going to cash in on it. It's not the first time some pretty little tramp has moved in and tried to take advantage of a rich old man's loneliness, but this one happens to have a family to protect his interests!"

Tally had angled around to where her hand was on the doorknob. She had to get out of here before she strangled on her own outrage, but before she went she had one more barrage to fire. "Some family! I'd sooner depend on a nest of rattlesnakes! What are you so worried about, anyway? Afraid he'll give away a few of those dollars you're panting to get your greedy hands on?"

Chapter Two

She was through the door before he could react. Shoes in hand, she fled silently down the broad staircase, almost coming to grief on the polished surface before she rounded the newel-post and dashed outside. The door swung to noisily behind her, and she didn't slow down until she was well clear of the deep, shadowed verandah.

Panting deeply in the hot, humid night air, she halted at the edge of the shelled driveway. She slipped her sandals back on her protesting feet, and then she straightened slowly as realization dawned on her. Both her purse and her overnight case were inside the house. The suitcase could wait, but how on earth was she going to get home at this hour of night without a cent of money? Well, *blast* the man for putting her in this position! He had probably done it deliberately, to punish her for being an amoral, gold-digging little tramp!

It took only the firm footsteps descending the steps behind her to galvanize her into action. Crushed shell crunched beneath her feet as she ran down the poorly lighted driveway. It was a hundred yards or more to the street over a badly maintained surface, and before she had gone half the distance her feet were in agony and she was covered by a fine film of perspiration.

The overpowering scent of night-blooming jasmine was almost sickening and she felt her senses reel. She slowed up, one hand clamped to her side to contain the shaft of pain brought on by exertion. Why couldn't he leave her alone! He had done his duty—she was leaving without having taken the silver or his uncle's life's savings!

"Wait!"

She started to run again, stumbling over roots that had encroached on the pale surface of the driveway. Her four-inch heels were half buried with each step, and she was gasping for breath when she felt steely fingers close over her arm with crippling force. She swore in exasperation, but the sound emerged as a soft moan.

"Where the devil do you think you're running off to?" Thane demanded, swinging her around to face him.

Stung by anger into a crazy sort of wildness, Tally cried, "Oh, I thought if I hurried I might be able to pick up some other lonely old man who'd offer me a fabulous illicit weekend!"

The clamp on her arm tightened until she winced. She'd be black and blue by morning, but darned if she'd let him know she was hurting! "Do it on your own time, then," he growled. "If you want to land in trouble of your own making I'd as soon not have to tell the police that I was the last man to see you before you disappeared! I have better things to do with my time than to have to go down to the police station in the middle of the night!"

A car cruised past, casting a flickering light through the ill-kept hedge, and Tally felt the last vestige of color leave her face. Thane, glaring down at her, suddenly released her arm and she rubbed it unconsciously, feeling the foolhardy resistance drain away as quickly as it had arisen. She turned away, head lowered, and began to pick her way over the rough surface. Oh, Lord, did he really think that of her? How had she gotten herself out on this impossible limb? Pride? Temper?

A little of both, plus a lot of tiredness and an ego that was permanently bruised from having been deserted first by her mother, then by her father, and now, from the looks of it, by her fiancé.

She lifted her head to tell him exactly how she came to be presiding at Hiram's table and then gave it up. It wasn't worth the effort. Thane Coulter meant nothing to her, his opinion was of less than no importance to her, and the sooner she saw the last of him the sooner she could forget this whole unfortunate, mixed-up episode.

"Come on, I'm driving you home." He caught her beleaguered arm again and she yelped, ducking under the pain. The man didn't know his own strength! Through his muttered apology, she blurted out that she was perfectly capable of finding her own way home.

She could as well have saved her breath, for he grabbed her arm again and dragged her back toward the house, with no consideration for her shorter stride or her highly unsuitable shoes. When they reached the car he had parked beside the house he opened the door, shoved her purse at her and poked her inside, slamming the door after her before she could mention her overnight case.

Oh, what the devil! She'd take the line of least resistance and get herself clear of any and all Coulters. Poor old Hiram would have to fend for himself, and she could call Mrs. Stoner tomorrow and have her case sent to her. At this point, her feet hurt and her arm hurt and she was bone tired. Besides, she wouldn't give this deep-frozen shark the satisfaction of arguing further.

"Where to?"

She gave her street number, added, "It's a block off Flagler," and settled back to enjoy whatever comfort she could on the ride home. The car wasn't a make she recognized, but from the surge of power that indicated the owner's temper, she suspected it was as powerful and aggressive as he was. Neither of them spoke on the twenty-minute drive, but more than once Tally's eyes strayed to the harsh, aquiline profile silhouetted against the passing streetlights. He turned suddenly to catch her staring, and she buried her gaze in her lap, snarling and unsnarling her fingers as she ached for the drive to be over.

They rounded the corner, and Thane slowed as Tally pointed out the house. It seemed even more uninviting than usual behind the leggy croton and the two discouraged-looking calamondins. Her talents didn't extend as far as landscaping—or rather, her time didn't.

"There are no lights," Thane observed grimly, pulling up to the curb.

"I forgot to leave one burning," she mumbled. She dug into her capacious bag for her key.

"Where's your family?"

None of your business, she thought irritably, but she was too tired to fire another shot. She told him tersely that they were on vacation.

"And while the cat's away . . ." he remarked mockingly, but then he added, "I'll step inside and look around."

Not for the world would she admit to herself, much less to him, that she hated walking into a dark, empty house by herself late at night. Instead, she walked silently to the door and unlocked it. Reaching inside, she switched on a battery of chrome-shaded lights, throwing Claire's newly decorated living room into garish relief.

Thane stepped inside, and she could almost swear he winced at the acid green carpet. He glanced around—almost, she told herself, as if he expected an assortment of men to come rolling out of the woodwork.

"Would you like me to check out the second floor?" He sidled past the big chrome and glass coffee table and glanced up the shadowed stairwell.

"I just want you to go," Tally agonized. Her hand was unconsciously rubbing her bruised arm, and tension made her eyes glitter helplessly as she stared at the man who seemed to fill the whole room with his presence.

Running a hand through the thick sun-bleached hair that contrasted so dramatically with the Coulter eyebrows, Thane said, "Look, Miss Fitzsimmons, I'm sorry if I hurt you. I don't make a practice of manhandling females, believe it or not." The words sounded as if they were actually forced from the strong, tanned column of his throat.

"Oh, don't you?" she retorted. "It must be a natural talent, then, because you do it quite effectively." She was amazed at how calm she sounded.

He winced. "All right, I deserved that, but I'd like you to accept my apology if I hurt your arm." Even if he was beginning to have second thoughts as to her character, that was apparently as far as he planned to go with his apologies.

"Mr. Coulter, I don't think it matters one whit to either one of us whether or not I accept your apology, because when you walk out of here in about two seconds, you can be certain that we've seen the last of each other! And furthermore, I doubt if either one of us will lose any sleep over the matter."

For a moment, she thought she had gone too far. The muscles that held that powerful body in a state of animallike readiness had tensed visibly, and then, with an indecipherable flicker of those Arctic eyes, he turned on his heel and left, slamming the door behind him with absolutely no regard for the sleeping neighbors.

Tally wilted where she stood, expelling her breath in one long, expressive sigh. She hadn't missed the tightening of those sensual lips, nor the angry flaring of his nostrils as he had given her that strangely shuttered look. Thane Coulter wasn't at all pleased at her refusal to exonerate him.

Well, that was just great! She slipped off her sandals and reached over her shoulder to begin unzipping her dress. He deserved an attack of conscience—that is, if the man even *had* a conscience!

It was pure habit that made Tally open her eyes shortly after six the following morning. As tired as she had been the night before, she had lain awake for hours mulling angrily over the whole preposterous misunderstanding.

Fiddle! Here she was, virtually on holiday, and still she couldn't sleep past her usual rising time. She stretched luxuriously, rolled over and smiled a sleepy good morning to David's picture. Impulsively, she lifted the photo and studied it, seeing the slender sweep of his long jaw, the thin nose and the arched eyebrows. It was almost a pretty face, although David would squawk long and loud if anyone hinted at such a thing. Certainly it was better looking than Thane Coulter's hardbitten one, with its arched nose, those heavy black brows and that rather wide, firm mouth with the disturbing hint of sensuality in the bottom lip. There had been lines radiating from the corners of his eyes and more across his wide, intelligent forehead that made him look older than the thirty-five years Hiram mentioned.

Impatiently, Tally forced her thoughts back to the face in the photo and then, as if it were a sort of lodestone, she touched her engagement ring. David was always the last thing on her mind at night and the first when she awoke, and it irritated her that last night's unpleasantness kept trying to interfere, like an insistent radio signal through a program of pleasant music.

Showering with an extravagant use of hot water and scented soap, she planned her day. First of all, a leisurely breakfast, a luxury in itself, since she was usually doing a load of laundry to be pegged out before she dashed off to work, or pushing the vacuum cleaner over Claire's new carpet while she munched her toast, pausing to sip coffee as she passed the table.

The dining room had been redecorated at the same time as the living room, but fortunately—at least from Tally's point of view—the kitchen was still the same old shabby-comfortable room, and it was here that she chose to enjoy her breakfast while she leafed through the *Post-Times*.

At this hour of Sunday morning, there was a welcome absence of traffic noise, and she took the various threads of sound—the squabbling birds in the mango tree, the lawn mower across the street—and wove them into a fantasy that was as familiar to her as the figures in her bedroom wallpaper.

Daddy was in the bathroom shaving and Mama was upstairs having coffee in bed before coming down to see Tally off to school. The rattling hum of the refrigerator was Daddy's electric shaver and the doorbell was . . .

The doorbell! Swallowing her dreamy smile, Tally jerked herself back to reality and scuffed around under the table for her slippers before dashing through the house to the front door. Who on earth could be leaning on the doorbell at this time of day? The sudden hope that no amount of disappointment could completely kill off faded away unnoticed as she stared blankly at the uniformed man on the front stoop. And then she saw her bright orange print overnight case in his hand.

"Miss Fitzsimmons? Good morning, miss. Mr. Coulter sent this."

He handed it over, touched the peak of his cap and spun off down the steps before she could even pull herself together enough to thank him.

"Thank you," she called out belatedly, as he fitted himself under the wheel of the elegant piece of machinery at the curb. It was neither the well-kept relic of Hiram's nor the dark red powerhouse Thane had driven her home in last night. A muted shade of gray, the Bentley or Rolls—she could never tell them apart—had purred away from the curb and rounded the corner of Flagler before she turned and went back inside.

Taking the same corner the following morning, Tally slowed to watch a black-hulled schooner pull away under power from the municipal pier. As always, whenever she relaxed the stern control she had over her thoughts, her mind flew on ahead to probe the horizon and beyond for a sturdy ocean-going tug named the *Elmira Queen.*

But that was almost three years ago. Her father could have changed berths half a dozen times since then. For all she knew, he might be captain of his own tug by now.

Before she could help herself, she slipped back to the days when a leggy, pig-tailed child had watched the big Trailways roll through Otter Creek on its way to Gainsville, willing it to stop with every fiber of her being, to stop and allow her mother to climb down that shiny step and sweep her up into a perfumed embrace again.

Not until she was thirteen had she learned that her mother was remarried and living in Ontario with her husband and her small son. By then Rex Fitz-simmons had met and married Claire on one of his shore leaves, and shortly after that they had moved from Otter Creek to West Palm Beach, to the house Claire owned from her first marriage.

Tally had lived for those times when Rex would arrive out of the blue, smelling of salt and rum and exotic places. For two weeks she'd be on her best behavior, hoping he'd decide to take her back to Otter Creek again instead of leaving her with a family that had small use for an awkward, introvert-ed stepchild—not that there was anything left for her there but memories.

He didn't, of course. The two weeks in, six weeks out gradually became one week in, two months out, and then a few days two or three times a year. Claire didn't seem to mind. She had her job in a North Palm Beach decorating shop and was determined to work her way out of the office and into the decorating part of the business. Judy had her own circle of friends, and she was preparing to go off to college. And so Tally stayed on, walking to high school, where she dreamed her way through academics and concentrated diligently on all the art courses she could fit in.

Her spare time was filled with household chores. Claire's career was in its infancy then, and with Judy getting ready to go off to school and no financial help from Rex, a maid was out of the question. Besides, it helped assauge her guilt at having been left on Claire's doorstep, so to speak. Tally even chipped in with a part of her meager pay from the child-care center. She really had no need to spend much on herself—she had little or no social life. Until she met David, that was.

But this was no time to be mooning about David!

Leaving the waterfront behind, she swung around the corner of Clematis and walked briskly to the office building. The past was behind her, the present only a stepping-stone to a future with David in Australia. If she hadn't heard from him by the time she had saved enough for her fare—with a bit left over for her keep—then she'd go anyway and start searching from his last known address. She'd soon convince him that there was no room in love for false pride.

According to Sara Drummond there were still no plums. Instead, Tally's week was spent helping a new mother bear up under the demands of a new baby, a new house, and two children under school age.

On the following Friday afternoon she returned to the office to let Sara know she was open for another assignment, since the mother-in-law had come to relieve her. Against all reason, the same old expectancy arose in her as she stepped off the slow elevator and turned toward the door inscribed HouseSpouse, Inc. Tally liked to think of herself as an optimistic realist, a sort of practical dreamer. She knew herself to be attractive, but she was certainly not beautiful. Though intelligent, she was no genius, and as for her artistic talent, it would never have amounted to more than a pleasant hobby, even if she had had the opportunity for further study. It did, however, color her point of view, enabling her to see loveliness instead of squalor, to see hope instead of hopelessness, and there had been plenty of times when that perennial optimism was all that kept her going.

"Still here?" she asked, peering in to see Sara dunk a cigarette in the remains of a cup of coffee.

"Whatever happened to weekends? I could swear there used to be a breathing space at the end of every other week! Come on in and clear out a perch. How was your workweek?"

"Jammy faces and untied sneakers, spit-up formula and, as if that weren't enough, a Lab puppy that was all ears, accidents, and appetite. Papa thought it would keep the kids from being jealous of all the attention the new baby got." She smiled in rueful remembrance and eased a foot halfway out of a neat navy blue pump.

"Men! Find one with a single thought outside his own comfort and convenience, and he's an idiot!" Sara's views on the male of the species were well known and equally well founded. She had supported her immature, unbelievably handsome actor husband by working at a Rent-a-Wife outfit on the West Coast until he snagged a part in a soap that shot him to instant stardom. At which point, he couldn't wait to shed everything connected with his former life—including Sara.

Tally's grin commiserated with her. Around Sara she tended to downplay her own good fortune in having become engaged to the only man she had ever loved. Or around anyone else, for that matter. Claire certainly had no patience for anyone else's romantic confidences—not after two husbands. And Judy openly declared her boredom with any man who didn't have a six-figure income. It grew harder and harder to find any common meeting ground with her stepsister, and sometimes Tally wondered why she even bothered to try.

"Anything on the books I could tackle this weekend, or shall I drop back on Monday morning?"

"As a matter of fact, your plum finally fell off the tree. Janice was practically drooling for a whack at it, but after just coming back from a two-week cruise with old Mrs. Potts, she had to step back to the end of the line. You're in—signed, sealed and ready to be delivered come Monday morning."

"If it's another cruise with some wealthy hypochondriac, I'd just as soon pass."

Sara twirled her red-rimmed specs. "What would you say to a two-week gig in Palm Beach with a live-in staff, a pool and whatever other perks you can scrape up for yourself? Not to mention no kids to chase after?"

"You must be kidding. Besides, with a live-in staff, what am I expected to do?" She had worked in well-attended places before in an executive capacity, but it always paid to ask first. There had been a few incidents over the past two years that she'd just as soon forget.

"The housekeeper sprained her back, as I understand it, and they're expecting a full house. Business entertaining, so there'll be wives to be kept occupied, the staff to order until the housekeeper gets on her feet again—you know the drill. Keep the food and drinks coming, the wives out of the way and the staff from walking out—especially with the silverware."

"That's no joke in some places. Remember the Kellermans? I walked in on the maid as she was stuffing her apron pockets with Mrs. Kellerman's pearls. Believe me, I wouldn't care to repeat that act!"

"Well, I understand the housekeeper and her husband, who chauffs, have been around since the flood, and the two maids are relatives. No problem there. Just cart the ladies around to the local attractions, turn and baste them occasionally around the swimming pool, and at the end of two weeks you'll be that much closer to Australia. Besides, it's past time you had a vacation. Honeymoons don't count."

"I can't imagine why not," Tally teased with mock innocence. "Claire and Judy won't be back for another week and a half, speaking of vacations. Do you think I can steal time to dash back home and check the mail and water Claire's plants? She paid a fortune for them and she'll have a fit if they droop."

"No reason why not. And while you're goofing off at fabulous wages, why don't you work on that tan you keep promising yourself?"

They laughed together at Tally's perpetual paleness and Sara's dusting of freckles, both offering to swap, and then Tally left, floating along the polished old linoleum to the elevator. She fairly danced along the sidewalk home. She hadn't even gotten the client's name, but what difference did it make? She was being picked up and delivered in style and she had a whole glorious free weekend before her.

She managed almost an hour in the sun on Saturday before the rains came, then she spent the rest of the day getting her clothes ready for a two-week stint on the other side of the tracks—which in this case meant the other side of Lake Worth.

On Sunday afternoon she gave Claire's houseplants a thorough soaking, thinking how utterly lacking in personality they were compared to Francis Coulter's cacti. But then Claire's sleek, glossy plants had been selected to accessorize her newly decorated rooms. Ungainly succulents that clambered all over the pots to lean drunkenly toward the sun weren't particularly sophisticated, no matter how endearing some people might find them.

When the doorbell sounded Monday morning, she was ready and waiting, dressed in her yellow cotton two-piecer with a daisy print scarf. Her black hair was brushed until the highlights fairly glinted from it, and her cornflower blue eyes held a sparkle of anticipation.

"Good morning," she said brightly, opening the door to the uniformed man who stood there, hat in hand. Her smile wavered uncertainly as she peered into the weathered face and then on beyond it to where a pearl gray Bentley—or was it a Rolls—waited at the curb. Something inside her lurched uncomfortably.

"Miss Fitzsimmons, I'm Hume. If your bags are ready?"

Because she couldn't think straight, she simply

glanced down at the two suitcases, and the chauffeur reached past her and picked them up, hopping lightly down the step to reach the car and hold the door open for her. Not until they were on the Flagler Memorial Bridge did she find her voice to ask where they were going, and then, when Hume mentioned a number on West Indies Drive, she was still no clearer.

Under her deceptively cool façade, turbulent thoughts fought for ascendency as they turned in between a pair of giant century plants and cruised slowly along a broad, curving stretch of driveway that was lined with white-boled royal palms. The house, modest in size only, was a classic design with Spanish tiled roof, set among flaming hibiscus and flamboyant trees against a somber background of Norfolk Island pines. Tally caught a glimpse of a pool and several outbuildings through the screen of shrubbery, but her attention quickly swung back to the enigmatic appearance of a broadly arched, slate gray door.

Swallowing apprehensively, she slid from the back seat as the uniformed man held the door for her. When he took her bags from the trunk and gestured for her to precede him, she couldn't withhold a doubtful look, and he grinned at her reassuringly.

"Go right on in, miss—you're expected. The missus is laid up, but we'll find one of the girls to show you to your room."

Tally, at that point, would have preferred to be shown the corner of Ninth and Flagler again, but she swallowed her nerves and allowed the chauffeur to usher her inside.

In the cool, spacious foyer, Hume put her bags down and nodded to a door farther along the corridor that extended back from the entrance. "I guess you'd better pop in and speak to the boss while I go locate one of the girls."

With a touch of his cap, he was gone, leaving Tally totally at sea. When no one appeared either to chase her out or invite her in, she gathered the spurious courage she borrowed for such occasions and marched to the door to rap briskly.

She would have recognized the voice anywhere, even if her bones hadn't already told her what to expect. Thane Coulter.

"Come in," he ordered, and she opened the door because she didn't know what else to do. There, across several acres of silky oriental carpet, across the gleaming surface of a broad fruitwood desk, sat the last man in the world she ever wanted to see again.

He was still wearing black and white, although today the white was a linen jacket and the black was an open-necked shirt that added depth and warmth to his mahogany skin. Thane Coulter nodded to her as if reaffirming something in his own mind. "Won't you have a seat, Miss Fitzsimmons?" He gestured to a dark green Queen Anne chair patterned with Chinese pheasants.

Tally opened her mouth to speak, realized she had nothing to say, and sat—but only on the very edge of the chair. Arranging her feet in prim alignment and clasping her hands in her lap, she waited for him to tell her what was going on. When he didn't speak, but continued to study her as if she were some *objet d'art* whose authenticity was in doubt, she took the initiative.

"Well?" she challenged, chin up and eyes flashing.

"Exactly," he nodded, his measuring gaze taking complete inventory of her person. He reached across the desk to remove the lid of a silver and ebony casket, selecting a thin cheroot. Carefully, he inspected it before clipping and lighting it, and Tally's head lifted by degrees, high color flowing into her cheeks.

"Now, Miss Fitzsimmons," he said finally, blowing a stream of blue, aromatic smoke aside, "I assume your employer told you what's required. My housekeeper picked an inconvenient time to throw her back out and I'm stuck with . . ."

"If you think for one single minute that I'm going to work for you, Mr. Coulter, then you're out of your mind," Tally broke in indignantly.

She began to rise and he barked at her. "Sit down!"

The sheer force of personality embodied in that commanding voice made her subside, but she was determined not to give one inch. It would take more than money to compensate for his insulting treatment of her. "Mr. Coulter—"

"Miss Fitzsimmons, I offered you an apology once before and you chose not to accept it." His eyes dropped to her upper arm, where his fingerprints had lingered for the better part of a week, and it was as if he had touched her. "Nevertheless, I'm offering it again. At the time I thought—well, you know what I thought." For just an instant his natural air of authority slipped, leaving him looking slightly ill at ease. "Believe it or not, there was every reason for my thinking what I did, although if I'd taken time to consider more carefully, I might have realized that you were cut from a different bolt of cloth from the other—ah—young ladies my great-uncle has seen fit to take under his wing. I know he's lonely," he continued, staring at the glowing tip of his cheroot. "Lord knows Uncle Francis is no company, and lately I've had my hands too full to drop by as often as I should, and when I did, there you were, all settled in for the duration. At least, that's how it looked from where I stood. I couldn't just stand by and see him taken for a ride again. And it's not the money, regardless of what you think," he added, leveling her a stern look.

Not that Tally had spoken a word of what she was thinking, but it was there on her openly skeptical face.

"A convenient birthday, a small loan so that they can go visit an ailing mother . . . whatever the ploy they use, the result is the same. Poor old Hiram forks over and then they're gone, leaving him a little bit sadder, but no less vulnerable to the next sweet-talking little tramp who turns up. Sometimes I think they pass the word around, like hobos and gypsies used to do years ago, with an esoteric symbol on the gate marking an easy sucker.

He stood then and moved restlessly around to the front of the desk, bringing him altogether too close for comfort. Tally preferred the expanse of polished wood between them to having that aggressively masculine frame leaning against the corner of the desk only a few feet away from her. There was something dangerous about him, about the obvious fighting trim of his tall, well-knit body as well as the less obvious, but nonetheless intimidating air of authority he wore with such careless ease.

"All right," she said grudgingly. "I can understand that, but that doesn't mean I'm going to work for you. I don't think we could get along, Mr. Coulter. Besides, there are plenty of people at HouseSpouse who'd be delighted to take over here in my place. Actually, I'm the least experienced one there. Most of the other women have kept their own houses for years. It's the ideal position for . . . for certain women," she broke off lamely. And it was. For the ex-homemaker back in the job market after years of being a wife, for grandmothers who needed a chance to be involved again, for women whose children had grown up and whose husbands had moved on to greener pastures.

"Mr. Coulter, I can personally recommend someone who'd be ideal for the job," Tally offered. Despite the fact that there was nothing even faintly threatening about the understated elegance of the fruitwood furniture, the hand-screened chintzes and the walls full of books and paintings, the room was closing in on her. Clutching her purse as if for protection, she stood up.

"Sit down, Miss Fitzsimmons."

"But—"

"Sit down!"

With that powerful figure looming over her she had little choice, but she glared up at him, determined not to allow herself to be intimidated . . . not again!

"Now, as I understand it, the contract I signed with your agency is as legally binding as any other such document. It specifies that I'm the recipient of your services for a period of two weeks, subject to renewal at the end of the initial term. Subject also to the usual stipulations as to time off, working conditions and that sort of thing."

He lifted one querying eyebrow and Tally found herself wondering if Sara had passed on the standing joke about the duties of a HouseSpouse; there were two things they didn't do, and one of them was housework.

"Now, if the decks are clear, we'll get down to particulars. Incidentally, it might interest you to know that Hiram not only peeled a strip off my hide over you, he rubbed salt in it. That was when I discovered who you were and where you worked. Then, when Mrs. Hume went 'down in the back,' as she calls it, it occurred to me that you were precisely what I needed—someone who was accustomed to stepping in and taking over in an emergency without missing a beat."

Gradually, as Thane explained the situation he found himself in with two couples arriving that evening for an extended stay and another to follow soon after, Tally found her anger seeping away. "The Evynses will be driving down from Hobe Sound. George's head of the firm's legal department and they live in Manhattan, where our main office is located, but Jessica's parents live here in Florida, so they'll stop over going and coming for a short visit with them. The Taylors will be arriving on the nine-twenty from Kennedy tonight. That's Thomas and Madelaine—you'll like them, I think. Tom's president of the firm. I'll expect you to take the women in hand, just pretend they're your own guests—you know the sort of thing women enjoy. Jess will have friends here, so she'll probably be pretty self-sufficient, but Maddie will need you."

"What is this firm—or don't I need to know?" Tally still had her reservations.

"Coulter International. We make oil recovery machinery, primarily." At that she perked up, and it was all the prompting he needed. As if he were more comfortable on familiar ground, he told her something about his firm. "With the rising importance of shale as a source, we're in a good position because we've been experimenting along those lines for some time. Up until recently, it hasn't been economically feasible, so a lot of our work at this stage is still strictly drawing board and prototypes."

When she continued to look at him expectantly, fascinated by anything faintly connected with David's field of mining, he went on to tell her that at the end of the first week he was expecting a representative from an Australian mining concern. "I understand he has family connections of some sort here in the Palm Beach area, so it was an acquaintance I was glad to renew. Recently there have been some big shale beds discovered in Queensland, and I think it would be a good idea to talk to these people—on an informal basis, of course. Thus the families—thus you." The cool gray eyes were momentarily transformed by a warming smile.

Three words were etched in Tally's mind: Australian mining concern. David had been in Queensland. True, Allied was bauxite, but mining was mining, and an Australian miner could give her some idea of where she might begin her search—in case she still hadn't heard from David by the time she had accumulated the fare.

"Meet me back here as soon as you've settled in and I'll show you around."

Chapter Three

Ushered into a stunning bedroom with an adjoining bath that was right out of the *Arabian Nights*, with its dark green marble and gold fixtures, Tally hardly had time to pause before she was being hurried along to meet the housekeeper. Mrs. Hume, a pouter pigeon of a woman, was thoroughly out of sorts at being laid up. She made no bones about the fact that she didn't expect much from a slip of a girl like Tally.

She was back at the study door in twenty minutes. Taking time to brace herself, she stood there, back straight and head unconsciously held high. She had a ready-made pep talk for such occasions—for times when she found herself wishing she'd chosen to package frozen fish at the processing plant, or trot along after Claire with a note pad and a tape measure in hand. What had ever given her the idea that it would be exciting to drop into the middle of other people's lives, take over the running of them for a few days, and then move on to some other set of circumstances? It was a living. It was a needed service, but it was also a gamble, and sooner or later, all gamblers drew a losing hand.

Resolutely, she opened the door and stepped inside. Thane was at his littered desk, those scowling brows meeting over his nose as he glared down at a list of figures. The scowl disappeared magically as he looked up and saw her, and when he smiled it was like the sun breaking through a bank of storm clouds.

Careful, girl. Don't go getting fanciful just because you like the cut of a man's jib.

"Ready?" He stood slowly, running a hand along the back of his neck as if to ease the tension there. "I'll give you an overview of the house, and you can ask questions as they come up, all right?"

It was a house filled with the sort of nooks and crannies a child would adore. Aside from the combination of study, library and office where they had started out, there was a lovely long sitting room called the East Room, where morning sun slanted through the lush greenery outside. There was an elegant formal dining room, and a comfortable, plant-filled room on the west side of the house, with jalousied windows, an assortment of lounges, and a wrought-iron table and chairs.

"I take most meals out here, but I guess we'll be having them inside for the duration. Maybe breakfasts here—what do you think?"

He honestly wanted to know? "I think it's a lovely place to have breakfast. With four guests, chances are they won't all be rising at the same time, so there'll be room. We'll see how it goes, all right?"

He took her to the guest wing, with its two

spacious bedrooms and two baths separated by a small sitting room, and then showed her a room that couldn't have been more than ten feet square. "Don't know what good this one is, but if you need a bolt hole, feel free."

There was a collection of mismatched furniture inside, including a table that could easily double as a desk. Tally decided on the spot that it would serve as her office. It had a good, solid door, and she had a feeling she might need a place to shut herself up and do a few deep-breathing exercises now and then. Her temper, dormant for ages now, seemed to be priming itself for a major awakening just lately.

Back in the East Room, Thane gestured to the doors that opened out onto the terrace and said, "Come on, you may as well meet MacGregor. He'll provide you with flowers for the house—*if* he happens to be in the mood. He's just as apt to accuse you of beheading them, though. They're his children, and he guards them jealously."

Again that smile, and Tally found herself wondering what Thane Coulter was really like. That first night, at Hiram's dinner party, he had been like a guard dog, bristling suspiciously at a stranger who had wandered into his territory. In the study, when he was telling her about his work, he had been a bit more relaxed, showing an unexpected side of his personality—the serious businessman. On the other hand, he certainly had what it took to be a jet set bachelor playboy—the looks, the bearing, the wherewithall.

And yet, oddly enough, he struck her as a man who was far more at home in a business setting than in a night club, more comfortable across a board room table than a roulette table. Or was she just being a bit more fanciful than usual?

Deliberately she turned her mind away from the man beside her and offered her hand to the wizened little gardener. She made no pretense of knowing anything about his specialty, but her enthusiasm was genuine enough when he showed her the rows of assorted flowers he called his cutting beds. "I'll see that ye have enough to get by with inside, but don't ye come a-cuttin' on ye're own, lassie. There'll be a bucketful inside the back door for ye to mess about wi' every morning, so keep out o' ma cuttin' beds, ye hear?"

She promised gravely, and they continued their stroll through the grounds. Thane grinned down at her as they passed the swimming pool and then they entered the house again through a small game room, complete with billiard table, card table and an inlaid chess table. The walls were hung with hunting bows, fishing rods and several trophy sailfish, and Thane leaned up against the edge of a glass-topped display case of antique firearms and grinned at her. "You passed muster, you know. Mac usually makes anyone wanting flowers crawl awhile before granting them a blossom or two, and you didn't even have to ask."

They had lunch on the jalousied porch, and over a delectable concoction of scallops, tomatoes and fresh corn, Thane told her about the running feud between the chef, Waldo, and the housekeeper. His clear gray eyes were fathoms deep and sparkling with laughter when he told her how Mrs. Hume had burned the chef's supply of paper hats that he wore in the kitchen as a badge of office, and how Waldo had retaliated by burning the housekeeper's favorite apron.

"The whole house reeked of burnt cloth for days,"

he chuckled. "I guess I ought to be grateful they didn't burn the place down."

Tally leaned back in her chair and laughed until tears brimmed her eyes. She had been slightly intimidated by the red-faced chef who looked more like a quarterback than a cook.

"So you can see why I need someone like you," he went on. His eyes lingered on her flushed cheeks speculatively, causing the flush to deepen—one of the hazards of her sort of coloring. "Do you know, that's the first time I've ever heard you laugh, Tally. It's a nice sound."

Her features quickly resumed their normally calm appearance as she drained the last of her iced tea. "Well, there's no reason why you should have heard me laugh, Mr. Coulter. After all, we don't really know each other at all."

He looked away, gazing absently out over the flawlessly kept grounds. "No, I suppose not. You just seem . . . I mean, I felt as if . . ." He moved his feet restlessly under the glass-topped table. "Perhaps it would be better if we forgot that first unfortunate meeting and started fresh. Could we do that, Tally?"

She was thrown completely off-balance. Thane Coulter—the insufferably arrogant, the unbearably condescending Thane Coulter—was ill at ease? With her? She felt as if she'd just grown five inches taller! "Of course, Mr. Coulter."

"Thane," he corrected. "If you're going to be living here, entertaining my friends and running my household, then we'd do better on a first name basis."

It didn't come easy. "Thane," she responded to his expectant look.

"Right. Now—suppose you tell me something about yourself. I've already told you my story."

He had told her a little about his work, but precisely nothing about himself. Evidently he was one of those men who didn't exist outside their work role. Somehow, she found that a little hard to believe. Even so, she couldn't go probing for all the details of his personal life, nor was she at all sure she wanted them. He could be charming, disarming even, and he certainly registered about an eleven on the Richter scale of masculine attractiveness.

Shuffling through the details of her very ordinary life, she said, "Well, I grew up in Otter Creek, over on the Gulf Coast—it's sort of southwest of Gainesville," she elaborated. "My father—" She didn't want to get into any of this, but one look at that jaw of Thane's and she decided she'd just as soon not risk another skirmish. "My father is a sailor. He's mate on an ocean-going tug out of Tampa. I live with my stepsister, who's a student at the University of Miami, and my stepmother, who's an interior designer. I . . . hmmm. I've worked in a day-care center part time since I was in high school, and—that's about it," she finished brightly.

His eyes seemed intent on peering into her head via her eyes. Maybe he didn't believe her, she thought with a return of her old antipathy. Maybe he was still suspicious of her. Maybe he thought she used her job to finger hot prospects for a ring of international jewel thieves!

And maybe you watch too much late-night television, she told herself astringently.

"Modestly reticent. Doesn't like to talk about self," he mused, a tinge of the familiar old mockery back in his voice. It was quickly gone. "That's the bare bones. How about fleshing them out a bit? Likes? Dislikes?"

"Allergies?" she chimed in, her hackles gradually settling down again under the spell of his contagious smile. "That's something I've learned to take into consideration ever since I planned a menu for a retirement party around lobster and the guest of honor was allergic to them. He spent the evening in the emergency room."

He grinned. "As far as I know, you're on safe ground here. Maddie hates chocolate and George is an Earl Grey drinker, but other than that, anything goes. How about you? You were going to tell me about your likes and dislikes."

"I was?" She was actually enjoying the badinage—which was a shame. It would be a mistake to find that she really liked this man. Nor did she care to dwell on the instincts underlying that conviction. "Likes. Hmmm . . . Well, I like mangos—and cheeseburgers all the way. I like art, but not the neat kind that looks like a photograph. I like music—"

"What kind?" He wasn't going to let her off that easily.

She frowned consideringly. "Bluegrass; Irish, of course; and the blatantly romantic composers. I don't care for crooners or rock, and I can't understand those serious modern composers who sound as if they'd stumbled into a hardware store with the lights off."

He laughed again and Tally was fascinated by the little lights that danced in the eyes she had once thought so glacial. "Books?" he prompted.

"Yep."

"Specifically?"

"Oh, I'm very democratic. I'll read anything from

Dr. Seuss to the fine print on back of the cough medicine bottle, but I really like C. S. Forrester sea stories. And if you're going to ask about allergies next, it's poison ivy, poison oak and poison sumac."

"I'll warn Mac to leave those out of his daily offerings." He stood up and held her chair, and they moved inside.

"I'd better go and see if I can get on working terms with your chef," she murmured, not wanting him to feel as if he had to entertain her further. After all, she was an employee.

"You forgot to tell me about this." He lifted her left hand and gazed at the small Tiffany-set diamond on her third finger. "When's the great occasion?"

Books and music were one thing, her personal life was another. On the verge of telling him just that, she glanced up to see a determined glint in his changeable eyes and she backed down. There was no point in starting off on the wrong foot—again. Not when she was going to be dealing with this man for the next two weeks.

Succinctly, she said, "His name is David and we're going to be married as soon as we save enough for a place to live. He—I—we're working on it. David's in Australia now, and I'll be joining him out there shortly. And now, Mr. Coulter—"

"Thane—please." He had forgotten to release her hand and she tugged it free, rubbing it against her skirt as if his touch burned her skin. Nor did he miss the instinctive action, unfortunately.

"All right, Thane. I'd better see to putting the finishing touches on the guest rooms and check on dinner, and then I promised Mrs. Hume I'd run over there to let her know how things were going. I think she hates being out of action." A small smile lighted her face and her eyes sparkled almost shyly up at his.

"I know she expects me to . . . what was her word? —bollux up the works?"

"In case you didn't know, Mrs. Hume has plans for the governor's mansion after she straightens me out, and then I think she might tackle Washington. According to her, they tend to bollux things pretty badly, too."

They parted on that genial note, and Tally found herself walking with the old spring in her step as she rounded the corner to the kitchen area. This wasn't going to be such a bad assignment, after all. And Thane was . . .

And Thane was about as predictable as a tornado. And potentially as dangerous. It paid to keep a wary eye on a man like that, she warned herself, not bothering to wonder at the source of her knowledge. Some things were gut-level reactions. Besides, she had seen him in action before. He could turn on the charm all right, but she'd seen him when the gloves were off.

It was after five before she saw a chance to escape to her room for a much needed shower and change. She had been going flat-out since she arrived. Even in a well-run household there were plenty of things to be done before the arrival of four houseguests. Mrs. Hume had been glad to turn the menu planning over to her, as she and Waldo never saw eye to eye, and Tally made arrangements for one of the girls to take meal trays over to the Hume's apartment.

Opening her door, she took time to study the luxurious room, noticing with surprise that it was even lovelier than the guest rooms. She had commented on the king-sized marble bath when the maid had shown her the suite earlier, but the girl had simply giggled and murmured something about Mr. Thane's instructions. She couldn't believe this was standard staff quarters, even in this choice neck of the woods.

Maybe he simply didn't want to emphasize the pecking order among the firm's employees by offering one of them much nicer accommodations. Not that tact and diplomacy were among his most outstanding qualities, Tally reminded herself with a small grin.

There were several large, flat boxes on her bed. Surely the first guests hadn't already arrived—she would have heard them. Unless they had come while she was on the phone hassling the market manager over the lobsters he had promised to deliver by four. The Evynses must have gotten in early, and the lobsters were late, and Faye—or was it Lucy?—must have forgotten and put the Evynses' things in here.

She stacked the boxes beside the door for now. Before she did anything else, she simply had to step out of her shoes and splash her face and neck and wrists with cold water. That had been her mother's discipline when, as a child, Tally's temper had gotten out of hand, but it was equally effective for cooling her body. Not even the air conditioning could keep her cool when she was going flat-out, and it took a lot of hidden effort to run a house of this size, even under ordinary conditions.

Of her employer she saw nothing at all until she heard him call to her from the foyer when the Evynses arrived. She had been settling a flap between Waldo and Lucy over the proper way to serve the soup course, confirming her worst fears about the inexperience of the girls. When she heard Thane's summons she was only too glad to escape the chef's burst of temperament.

"Come and meet our guests," Thane invited, extending an arm as if he expected her to walk into its circle. When Tally joined them, he introduced her to the tall, dark woman who had just greeted him with a lingering kiss, and to her husband, an austere man in lightweight tweeds that looked out of place in the tropical climate. She later learned that George Evyns was an Anglophile who dressed the part, even going so far as to affect a slight English accent. If Thane found it amusing, he showed no signs of it, mentioning later on that George was one of the top legal brains in the country when it came to international corporate law, and as such, could afford a few eccentricities.

Tally showed the Evynses to their quarters and returned to the East Room, as Mrs. Hume called the long, comfortable area with half a dozen full-length windows opening out into a terraced garden. Thane rose easily from the deeply cushioned chair and offered her a glass of sherry.

"All settled in?" he asked over the dry wine.

"They seem to be."

"How about yourself? Is everything to your liking?"

Placing her glass carefully on a delicate piecrust table, she nodded politely. Her gravely correct manner was compromised by the slightly myopic dreaminess of her large blue eyes. "Someone left some boxes in my room. Have you any idea where they belong?"

"They belong in your room," Thane replied matter-of-factly.

Tally raised her thin dark brows and waited for him to elaborate. In spite of his pleasantness, she had her doubts about this assignment.

"Didn't you open them?"

"Certainly not. What's inside them?" she couldn't resist asking.

She watched, puzzled, as Thane's expressive eyes gleamed with something resembling amusement. "Uniforms, I guess you'd call them. I had them sent out today, guessing at your measurements, so if they don't fit you can exchange them in the morning. Jess and Maddie both will enjoy an excuse to go shopping."

The constriction in her throat affected her voice, making it soft and small. "I see."

"Do you? I'm not so sure." He stood abruptly and moved across to a window, his broad shoulders in the dark knit shirt silhouetted against the filtered light that slanted through the Norfolk Island pines. Turning abruptly, he leveled a searching look at her. "Tally, all my staff wear uniforms, but not because I insist on it. Either they like the looks, or the convenience, or—well, whatever. At any rate, I'm expected to provide them with suitable clothing as long as they're in my employ. Do you understand?"

Wrapping herself in a cloak of hauteur, she said, "Certainly, sir." Not for the world would she reveal the wounding effect his words had on her. Oh, it was all very well to keep reminding herself that she was merely another paid employee in the Coulter household, but a uniform!

Well, at least, she thought bitterly, if she were inclined to forget her position when Thane was in one of his more democratic moods, handing out glasses of his best sherry, her uniform would remind her.

"What did you say?" His words were dangerously soft, his anger baffling, and she could only stare at him blankly, wondering how she had managed to transgress this time.

"I said I do understand, Mr. Coulter," she enunciated stiffly.

Looming over her, he uttered one short, impolite word before lifting her by the elbows and practically suspending her before him. "Let's get one thing straight, Tally Fitzsimmons," he rasped. "The name is Thane. Go on, say it!"

The dark glitter of his eyes almost paralyzed her but she got the word out past stiff lips. "Th-Thane."

He didn't release her. Instead, he continued to stare at her, his gaze moving palpably over her short straight nose, her rounded chin, and lastly her lips, which had an unfortunate tendency to tremble under the intimidation of his stare. "That's better," he murmured absently, as if his mind were anywhere but on his words.

Releasing her suddenly, he stepped back, his head lifted in that unconsciously arrogant attitude so characteristic of him. "Why don't you go and change for dinner. No point in waiting for the Taylors; they'll probably have dinner on the flight. Take a rest if you want to—there's time."

He turned away, and considering herself dismissed, Tally could hardly wait to escape. Once outside the room, she expelled her breath in one long gust. Never in her life had she met anyone who could throw her out of countenance so quickly! It had taken ages to build up her self-esteem after her mother had left, and she had had to work on it time and time again in the past few years. Without even trying, this man could fracture her thin layer of poise and play havoc with her emotions, and it didn't make any sense. It didn't make any sense at all!

Hurrying along to her bedroom, Tally automatically noted the flowers she had arranged for the hunt table. MacGregor had come through handsomely. Tally had just finished the flowers for the dining room when the flap in the kitchen broke out. She only hoped no one was allergic to the daliahs she had placed in the two guest rooms. She had chosen scentless blossoms, preferring that sort herself for her own room. Not that she had had that many flowers in her bedroom. She felt fortunate to be able to enjoy the sun-drenched scent of clean linen and fresh air. If Claire had her way, the laundry would be dried in the drier and the windows all closed in deference to the air conditioner.

Entering her room, Tally went directly to the long mirror and studied her reflection. She had put on a nice-looking pastel cotton with a touch of schiffli embroidery on the collar. Was it so objectionable? It seemed a terrible extravagance to have to buy uniforms for someone who'd only be here two weeks, but if that was what Mr.— And that was another thing! *Thane.* Thane, indeed! She hadn't heard Faye or Lucy or Hume calling him by his given name, nor had she heard him reprimanding them for their formality.

Lips clamped tightly together, she stalked across to the boxes she had stacked beside the door and picked up the top one. There were an awful lot of them, and the name . . . Recognizing the logo of one of the best-known establishments on Worth Avenue, one she was reasonably sure did not cater to household staff, she undid the catches and folded back the layers of white tissue suspiciously.

"Ooooh!" It was almost a groan. Instinctively, she reached out to touch the zephyr-soft fabric, a chiffon in misty blends of blue and violet with a silver-green tracery of fern. Rejecting the impulse to hold the dress up for further inspection, she opened another, and then another, until the bed was strewn with tissue and elegant cartons and a rainbow of dresses, both long and short, as well as a couple of bathing suits and two pairs of slacks with matching silk shirts.

It was a good thing there was a chair behind her, because she simply dropped. Oh darn, oh blast! Was this some sort of cruel joke? Surely not even Thane Coulter would be this insensitive! The man couldn't seriously expect her to calmly accept hundreds of dollars' worth of clothing.

Hundreds? The chiffon alone was worth that!

He was testing her. That was it. Agency or no agency, Thane had still not stopped suspecting her of any of the guilty motives he had laid at her door that night over a week ago.

Well, we'll just see about that! Snatching up the chiffon as if it were a thrift-shop special, she marched across the silencing celadon carpet and flung open her door. Anticlimactically, the East Room was empty, and she glanced into the study where she had first encountered him this morning. Some of her righteous anger was transposed into bafflement by that time, and she turned to Hume, who was crossing the foyer with the keys to the Evynses' car.

"Do you know where I can find Mr. Coulter?"

The tall, weathered chauffeur glanced curiously at the bundle of delicate fabric in her hand and nodded his head. "I expect he's gone to change for dinner, miss."

"And where is that? It's important," she added, seeing the peculiar look the man was giving her. Surely he didn't think . . . ?

"His room's the one adjoining yours, miss." Evidently taking her stunned look for disbelief, he assured her that Mr. Coulter's room could be reached from her bathroom or through the second door down the hall.

By the time she reached the ivory-paneled door she was livid. Taking a deep, steadying breath, she rapped sharply and waited, her foot beating silently on the faded Tabriz runner.

"I thought it was about time," Thane said as he swung the door open to reveal the honey-toned paneling beyond. His room, she saw at a glance, was designed to harmonize with hers. Both used the pale green carpet and deep green appointments, his offset by the warm paneling, while her own walls were covered in creamy silk.

Face to face with the man, she could think of no words that could adequately express her feelings. They went beyond mere anger. She was deeply hurt to think that after all the fine words he had spoken, after all the confidence with which she had taken over the reins of his household and greeted his guests, he was still only playing some underhanded game to make her admit she was—to put it crudely—on the take.

She thrust the gown at him. "Waldo has the meal plans for the next three days and Mrs. Hume should be able to manage if you fix her a cot in that little room off the kitchen," she said coolly, never so polite and correct as when she had been hurt to the quick.

Ignoring the dress, he caught her wrist and yanked her back into the room, wrecking the fragile framework of her dignity. "All right, all right, it's not what you obviously think, but honestly, Tally, I just didn't know how to handle it! You'll admit it's a delicate situation—offering a woman clothing without either insulting her or compromising her. It's purely a straightforward business transaction, but I knew I could count on you to misunderstand!"

"I don't think there's much to misunderstand," she said stiffly, heels together and arms held rigidly at her sides. The chiffon trailed unheeded on the floor. "You move me into your house, into a room that adjoins your own, and—stash all this *loot* in there when I'm not looking, and then you—you . . ." When her voice began to waver she broke off and glared at him through drenched eyes.

Pressing his fingers to his temples, Thane sighed. In spite of her own distress, it occurred to Tally that the gesture made him look remarkably weary, even vulnerable. But appearances were all too deceiving, as she had good reason to know, and she refused to be tricked into feeling sympathy for a man who delighted in manipulating people for his own amusement. All set to leave the room, the house, and the job, she was halted by one softly spoken word.

"Please."

She paused, her back to the man who had spoken. Not that she was taken in by his act. Still, she was aware of a strange, compelling feeling growing inside her at the thought of a man like Thane Coulter actually begging.

And amazingly enough, he *was* begging. "Please stay, Tally, and let me at least try to explain my motives. I don't deserve your consideration, I know, after the way I lit into you at Hiram's house, but I think you're a good deal kinder than I am. I can only hope you'll give me the benefit of the doubt, even though I withheld it from you that night."

What could she do? He led her to a cinnamon-colored suede chair and she sank into it, still clutching the offending evening dress. She lifted it hastily and made some effort to fold it as Thane paced the floor before her, obviously at a loss as to how to begin now that he had her attention.

"The rooms?" she prompted, instinctively wanting to help him out of his misery. She doubted very much that Thane Coulter had much experience at apologizing and explaining.

"The rooms. Would you believe simple logistics? Each of the two guest rooms has an adjoining bath. This suite has two bedrooms and a single bath. If I gave either the Taylors or the Evynses the room adjoining mine, that would mean three people queuing for the bath. When one of the contenders is female, that compounds the ratio all out of reason. No offense to your sex intended—it's just a fact of life. Women take longer. There's always something that needs rinsing out, I guess."

A bubble of amusement rose to the surface and she suppressed it.

"If, instead, I gave the adjoining room to you, that would mean only two of us fighting over the territory, and it just didn't occur to me that you'd see it in another light."

It made sense. She admitted it reluctantly. The house, for all its quiet luxury, was small. Just right for a couple, or a single man, but when the population expanded several hundred percent overnight, some shuffling around was to be expected. "All right," she conceded. "I understand that, but the clothes. Surely you don't expect me to accept these—these . . ." Helplessly, she held up an edge of the gossamer fabric.

Thane ran a large square-tipped hand through his hair. "Look, when I told you about uniforming my staff, I wasn't trying to mislead you, Tally. You are—well, in a way, you're a member of my staff, although I prefer to think of you as a friend pitching in in an emergency."

Tally sagged and sighed in exasperation. These Coulter men and their overweening pride! Did they have a congenital blind spot? If it was so all-fired important for them to have help now and then for entertaining, then why not admit they had hired a hostess or an executive housekeeper for the duration? "I hadn't noticed Mrs. Hume wearing anything quite so frivolous," she said dryly.

"Maybe it's just a case of a difference in tastes," Thane pointed out, not without a gleam of humor in those changeable gray eyes. "Mrs. Hume selects the uniforms for all the staff, but I sort of wanted to have a go at choosing yours myself. Did I go too far off the beam?"

She had to laugh at that. The whole thing was so ludicrous now that she took it apart and analyzed it, but there was still just that small twinge of hurt. "I take it you don't care for my taste in clothes."

Dropping down into the chair that matched her own on the other side of a drum table, Thane said, "Look, Tally, not to mince words, I've known Jess for a long time. She's a smart woman and a good friend, but she can be a bit of a—well, she can be pretty scathing on occasion." At her look of surprise, he went on, "Oh, don't think all men are taken in by a woman's subtle cattiness. I employ at least as many women as I do men, and believe me, any man who underrates them—in *any* respect—is in for trouble."

Tally didn't know whether to be amused or incensed for her own sex. There was obviously more to Thane Coulter than met the eye, and what met the eye was almost too formidable for her own comfort.

"You mean Mrs. Evyns might not approve of my clothes?"

"I mean I expect you to take Jess and Maddie—as well as any Cartwright women, if and when they arrive—in hand and keep 'em out of sight while we iron out the wrinkles in the Cartwright deal. If I know Jess, that means the Swordfish Club, Cartiers, Saint Laurent's and all the rest, with the necessary resuscitation breaks at Elizabeth Arden's. I want you armed to the teeth, so that if you find yourself spending a lot of time with that crew of hedonists she runs around with here, you won't be made uncomfortable. In other words, you'll be more effective if you're properly dressed for the assignment."

"You want me to blend in with the natives, in other words," Tally suggested dryly. She idly pleated the fabric in her lap. Taken in that light, she supposed it made sense; all the same, no woman likes to be told that her own clothes are unattractive.

Reading her thoughts accurately, Thane said, "It's not that you don't always look lovely, Tally—you do. That blue thingumabob you had on at Hiram's was fine, but you don't set a diamond in brass without losing a lot of its effectiveness. And I'm paying you to be as effective as possible, so it's only simple business logic to provide you with the best possible tools."

She didn't know whether to be pleased at the diamond bit or insulted at the brass. "Well, if you put it that way— All the same, it doesn't seem right to go to The Esplanade when you can find some pretty things across the bridge at a fraction of the cost."

"Relatively speaking, those things I had sent out were to my salary what the blue dress was to yours. Now, I think we've wasted enough time on this nonproductive subject and we need to get dinner out of the way before we pick up Maddie and Tom, so . . . I'll toss you for first shower, all right?"

"If you can be magnanimous, then so can I," Tally said grandly. "You go first, and please—take all the time you need." She swept from the room with a wicked grin. She had already showered, and besides, she was going to be well occupied for the next half hour or so, trying on all her new finery.

Three days later, returning to her room after the others had settled down for bridge, Tally was grateful to Thane for his insight into Jessica Evyns's character. She slipped the straps of a royal blue silk from her shoulders, stepping out of her shoes at the same time. The gown was casually styled, with wide straps and large patch pockets, making the exquisite fabric all the more striking.

That first night they had not dressed for dinner, and last night George and Jessica had dined with friends, leaving Thane and Tally to entertain the comfortably middle-aged Taylors. Maddie Taylor was a tall, enthusiastic woman who could talk art with Tally or sports with her husband without missing a beat. She endeared herself to Tally immediately by confessing that she never left the table without feeling a compulsion to scrape the plates and carry them out. Tom had not always been president of Coulter International, and Maddie made no pretense of being to the manor born, as did the Evynses. But of course, with George and Jessica it was no pretense.

Wriggling her toes in relief, Tally lifted David's photo from the rosewood table beside her bed. "I'm going to have to borrow from our fund, darling," she confided to the handsome face that gazed back at her so gravely. David tried hard to look older than his twenty-five years, but the very refinement of his features lent him a certain delicacy that would always make him look young. "It's either that or go begging from that man, and I'd do without first."

For all her lovely new things, she was still hobbling about in her worn-out silver sandals. It was either those or the navy pumps, and the two blues were all wrong for each other; nor could she see stacked heels and top stitching with slubbed silk. A pair of inexpensive shoes wouldn't break her, for goodness sake. She'd consider them a part of her trousseau, and in light of the fact that she had unexpectedly acquired most of that, she could indulge herself with no guilty feelings at all.

Rubbing the sole of her foot absently, she rationalized. The Cartwrights just might be able to cut short her search once she got to Australia, thus saving her enough so that she and David could set up somewhere on their own, even if it was only a two room apartment. At least Mr. Cartwright might be able to give her an idea of where to start looking for a mining engineer who specialized in bauxite. There couldn't be that many choices, surely, unless David had branched out into another field altogether. There was tin, nickle—Australia abounded in minerals, she remembered with a sinking feeling, and David's restless streak just might have overruled his common sense.

Voices from the game room farther along the terrace came clearly through her open window. Lying in bed, Tally could hear Jessica's rather irritating drawl as she passed judgment on several mutual friends for Thane's amusement. Not that he sounded especially amused, to give him credit. It hadn't taken

Tally long to learn that Jess Evyns preferred the company of men in general, and Thane in particular. Even so, Tally couldn't help but admire the striking stylishness of her lean, dark good looks. Only a woman who was utterly secure could wear her frosted hair in such a severe cut.

Until tonight, Tally might just as well not have been present, for all the attention Jess paid her. Tonight, for some reason, it had amused the older woman to take a special interest. "Where did you attend school, Miss Fitzgerald?"

Tally had watched her flick the ash from her after-dinner cigar into one of the Sevres cups. Without bothering to correct the error, Tally mentioned the high school she had attended, knowing full well that this was not what the other woman had meant. That elicited a lift of penciled brows, and the next question had concerned her home. "You're—ah—visiting, I understand. Just where did you say your home was?"

Thane made a move to adjourn, but with an odd feeling of perversity, Tally said quite clearly, "I live over in West Palm." She mentioned the street and watched the acrobatic eyebrows go into action again.

"Oh, really? How odd." She glanced at Thane and then smiled sweetly at Tally. "One would think you'd want to go farther afield for your vacations, but then I suppose this is like a different world to you, isn't it?"

It was Thane who mentioned the condominium that had recently been built near Tally's street. "As a matter of fact, I've been trying to get Hiram to close up that anachronism of his and move into one of the condos over there. Then maybe between us, Tally and I could manage to keep him out of trouble." His lazy grin was aimed at Tally, but she knew it was meant to defuse Jessica's inquisition. She should have appreciated it; for some reason, she didn't.

Rising with a restless motion, the older woman had announced, "I'm in the mood for some cut-throat bridge. Who has a taste for punishment tonight?"

When Tom had declared his intention of watching the tennis matches on television, Jess hooked her arm through Thane's and gave him the full benefit of her slow smile. "We're a team, darling. Let George put that cunning brain of his to work and see if he can hold Maddie's nose above water."

Tally had lingered to see that the girls cleared everything away as swiftly as possible. Not that she expected them to linger over the last chore of the day, not when their dates were waiting.

It was too early to go to bed. With the French door open into the soft, fragrant night, Tally found herself growing oddly restless, in spite of being achingly tired. She had had to keep a close eye on Faye and Lucy to get the rooms done properly, and at least half a dozen times she had had to dash over to the Hume's apartment to confer with the house-keeper. And then she and Maddie had spent the afternoon touring the galleries and several of the public gardens.

Breathing a mild oath, she swung her feet out of bed and moved silently to the open window. Farther along the terrace the voices of the bridge players rose and fell against the sound of distant traffic, and Tally's gaze lingered on the light that streamed from the game room. She didn't play bridge, not that anyone had invited her. But she swam. And the pool glittered invitingly through the screening shrubbery. With no conscious thought, she made a decision.

A few minutes later, the marvelously soothing water closed over her head and she swam the length of the pool before surfacing, then rolled over on her back and gazed up through spangled lashes at the stars. They looked like all the diamonds in the world tossed carelessly across a blanket of black velvet, and she began to try to organize them into various constellations.

Paddling lethargically when she drifted too close to the edge, she wondered what the Southern Cross looked like, and if, by chance, David was gazing up at it and thinking of her. It almost worked. The bond she had thought unbreakable had been stretched just lately until sometimes she thought the tension was all gone, like a worn-out rubber band, but now it pulled her back and she could almost hear David's voice, see his face.

Almost. Instead, a lean, angular face with a proud nose and ebony eyebrows under a thatch of moonlight-pale hair intruded on her daydream, and she snorted impatiently and rolled over on her face. Floating face down, her hair a dark cloud on the darker surface of the unlighted pool, she held her breath as if it were a penance of some sort. Just before she lifted her head to expel it, her fingers touched the smooth tiles at the edge of the pool and then her wrist was clasped in a bone-crushing grip. She felt herself being hoisted out of the pool, raked ruthlessly against the edge, and she swore loudly.

"Don't you *ever* pull a stunt like that again!" He was kneeling beside where he had dropped her unceremoniously on the hard tiles.

"I was not pulling any stunt! I was floating!"

"Then float with your face up from now on! Better still, stay out of the pool unless someone's with you! Is that clear?"

"I don't have to swim in your blasted pool at all! Why don't you post signs?—off limits to the hired help!"

Catching her under her arms, he stood up, his fingers biting into her ribs. The angle of those heavy brows was enough to tell her that he was furious, without the ragged sound of his breathing. Tally tossed the heavy burden of her wet hair back from her face and glared back at him, oblivious to the intoxicating scent of tropical flowers and the soothing sounds of the nearby ocean. A mixture of anger, embarrassment and something too alien to recognize made it impossible for her to speak, and she spun away and headed for her room.

Chapter Four

Thane's longer stride brought him silently to her side before she had covered half the distance, and he caught her by the arm, swinging her around by her own momentum. Tally was slammed against the dry warmth of his dinner jacket and she shoved against him.

"What are you running for?" he demanded.

"I'm not running!"

They were out of range of the house lights, and she deliberately hadn't turned on the pool lights. It was impossible to read his face. "No?" The one word was enough to set off alarms in her defense mechanism. Her answering negative was barely audible.

Thane's hands slipped down over her shoulders to her back, sliding easily over her wet skin. He drew her closer to him and Tally pressed her hands against his chest, half dazed by the glittering tension that streaked between them. She felt vulnerable in a way she had never felt before and it was frightening.

Without relinquishing his hold on her, Thane lifted her left hand and brought it to his face, spreading the palm over his cheek and covering it with his own hand. "Your hand is cool. What's that old saying about cool hands?"

"I don't remember," she murmured, remembering very well.

"You don't wear your engagement ring when you swim?"

Still entangled in the shadowy mystery of his eyes, she said, "I'd already gone to bed, but I couldn't sleep. I—I don't wear my ring to bed."

"Hmmm . . . I wonder if there's anything Freudian in that. Your young man's in Australia, I believe you said. Has he been gone long?"

She had told him that much, little more, and certainly not the fact that she had temporarily lost contact with David. Nor had she mentioned the fact that she planned to pump his Australian guest the first chance she had. If he didn't care to have the staff make use of his pool, she knew darned well he'd have fits if he knew she planned to make use of his precious Mr. Cartwright! Avoiding the issue, Tally backed away, shivering in spite of the still, warm air.

"You're going to catch a chill," Thane said, a disturbing gentleness deepening his voice. "Better run along and dive into a hot bath. You've just about enough time before I come banging on the bathroom door." She could see the gleam of his white smile in the near darkness and it rattled her even more than the unexpected note of kindness. She didn't expect that sort of thing from Thane Coulter. She didn't *want* it!

"Yes—uh, all right. I will," she muttered, backing away. Before she could turn from him, however, he reached out and captured her face between his hands.

"Good night, child," he whispered, and lowered his face to place his lips on hers in an incredibly tender salute.

Thanks to sleeping on damp hair, Tally decided she looked like a sheep dog in need of a trim when she joined the women for coffee the next morning. She had been up for well over an hour, and had already had her breakfast in the kitchen while she went over the day's menu with Waldo.

Jessica greeted her with a jaded glance. "Rough night? Maybe I can bribe my hairdresser to undertake a rehabilitation job. Your sort of hairstyle can look so terribly . . . *ordinary* in the hands of an amateur."

"Thanks," Tally replied, surface politeness covering an inward grimace, "but I promised to go biking with Maddie this morning. We're going to take a picnic up to the north end. Any rehabilitation job would be wasted." Tally was quite sure the word "ordinary" had been substituted for another, even less flattering word. At least her hair didn't look as if it had been spray painted onto her head!

Maddie spoke up with typical tact. "Last year Tom and I were out in the inlet with Thane on his boat, and I almost saw a wild parrot. This time, darn it, I'm determined to see one for myself, and I'm taking my camera along, too."

The men joined them at the table as Jessica drawled. "Tell me, darling, how does one *almost* see a parrot? Either you did or you didn't."

Tom answered for her. "Poor Maddie," he

laughed. "I spotted the thing and pointed it out to Thane, and he yelled down to Maddie to look out a-starboard, and she—"

"And by the time I figured out which was starboard, the blooming thing was gone—*if* they ever actually saw it. My oldest grandson wants a snapshot of either a parrot, an alligator or the creature from the sleepy lagoon."

Tom swatted his wife on the behind and straightened her out on the jumbled titles, and Thane told Tally that Hume would give them a lift to the bike rental shop and pick them up there later on. There was nothing in his manner to indicate that he even remembered having kissed her good-night, and she forced herself to meet his enigmatic gaze with the same equanimity.

It was midafternoon before they returned from their expedition. They turned in the bikes and Tally phoned Hume and then joined Maddie on the bench outside the shop. They watched the scattering of tourists sauntering past, and the procession of luxury cars, all tightly sealed against the hot afternoon sunshine. Tally pointed out a nearby gallery, and Maddie mentioned one of the paintings in the dining room that she had always liked as having belonged to Thane's mother. While Tally listened with carefully disguised eagerness, the other woman went on to talk about Thane's parents.

"The house was theirs, but before they left on a world cruise, they moved over to the Towers. It's easier to keep up with than a house and grounds."

"I'm sure it is," Tally murmured.

"You knew, of course, that Gus, Thane's dad, retired after his last heart attack. He turned the house over to Thane, along with the chairmanship and the killing responsibility that goes with it. I hate to see Thane go the route his father took, driving himself seven days a week, fifty-three weeks of the year—especially when his heart's not really in it."

Tally looked at her questioningly, absently stroking her pink thighs. She didn't tan at all easily; either she burned or she took it slow and easy, and since she seldom had time for the latter, she invariably ended up looking parboiled after an impromptu outing.

"Being a theoretical engineer, he'd much rather be in the design end of the business, but after his father's first coronary accident Thane went back to Harvard and added an MBA to all those fancy degrees from Cal Tech, so that Gus would slow down and let some of the weight fall onto his shoulders. Gus held on, though, until it almost killed him. Thane asked Tom to move up to chairman of the board, but Tom refused. Thank goodness."

Catching a glimpse of the Bentley rounding the corner, Tally gathered the basket with the remains of the picnic in it. "You didn't want him to?"

"I didn't even want him to take the presidency. Tom will be sixty-four in March, and that's no time to be piling on responsibilities. Besides," she added candidly, "I want him to have some time for us while we're still young enough to enjoy it."

As they strolled out to the waiting car Tally hastily revised her assumption that romance was only a memory for Maddie and Tom. Maddie, catching her speculative look, laughed.

"Oh, I know, I used to think the same thing, with all the blind arrogance of the very young; but believe me, honey, love, like everything else, gets better with practice. With the right one, the older you get, the more your capacity to love and be loved increases, and I'm not speaking just of sex . . .

although that, too. On the rare weekends when Tom's home and the house isn't overrun with grandchildren, well—all I can say is, the honey still flows."

With Maddie's words echoing in her ears after she had gone to bed that night, Tally lay awake and wondered if someday she and David might find such fulfillment. She considered the painful examples of marital strife in her own background—her father and his two wives, and Claire and her two husbands. Four people and not a single successful marriage as far as she knew. There was Sara, too. No wonder so many people were wary of commitments. She wished David could meet the Taylors.

By morning the pinkness of her thighs had faded and she was back to her usual pale self. Thane noticed it at breakfast. "Why don't you girls spend a quiet afternoon at the pool, and then we'll knock off early and try out the band at the Swordfish. I think you've earned some sort of reward for being extremely patient all week."

Jessica was gone all morning and opted out of the quiet afternoon, choosing to keep a tennis date. Maddie went off on her own after breakfast to shop for her grandchildren in the morning while Tally set about earning her salary. In spite of the fact that she had a full staff—or perhaps because of it—there never seemed to be a lack of things to do to see that all gears meshed smoothly. She might have felt guilty about spending so many enjoyable hours in such plush surroundings except that somehow, she wound up exhausted by the time she fell into bed each night.

"Better oil up," the older woman warned that afternoon offering Tally some of her own preparation. "You'd be better off staying in the shade altogether. Believe me, by the time your skin's soaked up sixty years of sun, it's too late to go back and use a little common sense. You just have to look leathery and like it."

"You look anything but leathery," Tally murmured sleepily. "With that gorgeous hair for contrast, you'd make a great model."

"Deliver me! Can you imagine a more deadly existence than spending your life changing clothes?" Maddie laughed.

"My stepsister's a model. At least she's a student at the University of Miami, modeling part time, but I expect she'll end up making a career of it. She has the looks."

"To each his own." Maddie shrugged. "Poke me if I start to fry. I think I'll doze awhile if we're going dancing tonight."

Carefully smoothing a protective lotion over herself, Tally settled down on her stomach to leaf through a travel magazine. She had read about a third of an article on the Great Barrier Reef of Australia, her mind straying off on a delightful tangent that included a honeymoon there with David, when the glare from the glossy page became too much for her. Her eyelids drifted down, her head turned to the side and settled comfortably onto the cushion, and her finger trailed between the pages of the forgotten magazine. A fine film of perspiration bathed her as the sun bore down on her back.

It was the housekeeper who awakened her. Mrs. Hume, with the help of a heavy support garment, was beginning to get out for a few hours each day, and she had been on her way back to her apartment over the garage when she caught sight of the two sleeping women.

"Miss Tally, you ought to know better, and you

Florida born," she scolded. "I've seen some foolishness in my day, but this beats the lot! How do you think you're going to carry on with a back like that? Child, you won't be fit to soak beans for the next few days!"

Already Tally was discovering the truth of her charge. Lifting her head from the flowered cushion was enough to cause the tender skin of her nape to wrinkle agonizingly. She yelped. Hearing the commotion, Maddie stirred from her own lounge, which was now in the shade of the poincianas, thanks to the progress made by the sun while they both had slept. The older woman brushed a few scarlet blossoms from her lap as she sat up.

"Uh-oh! Looks as if I fell down on the job, and after all my words of wisdom." She glanced ruefully after the rigid back of the housekeeper as it disappeared into the apartment entrance. "Lordy, honey, you're burned to a frazzle. What happened?"

"I guess I—ouch!—dozed off. Maybe it won't be so bad once I shower and smooth some lotion on it. Yesterday's dose had all soaked in by this morning, remember?" She winced, feeling around on the hot tiles for her scuffs. From a long past history of just such accidents, she knew darned well she'd be miserable for days, but not for the world would she allow Maddie to take the blame. Tally was a native of the Sunshine State, and certainly too old to need the services of a nursemaid!

By dinnertime she knew she was in no shape to go dancing. If she managed to get dressed and sit at the table without a perpetual grimace on her face, she'd be doing well. She made herself supervise the preparations for dinner and arrange fresh flowers for the table, and she managed to talk to Waldo about a menu for children, just in case it was needed. There had been some mention of a flying trip north with the Cartwright man, leaving his family under Tally's wing, and she had no idea whether the children were at the bib-and-bottle or the hamburger-and-French-fry stage.

She wore one of her own dresses—one Judy had passed on after discovering that the olive, purple and gold paisley made her appear sallow. It didn't look any too flattering to Tally's multicolored hide, either, but then nothing would flatter a face that was sickly pale on one side and burned to a livid cerise on the other, thanks to her habit of sleeping on her stomach with her head turned to the side. At least the silky fabric and the caftan styling slithered on over the minimum of undergarments without causing any extra agony.

Joining the others for predinner drinks, she accepted her usual dry sherry, needing the stimulant rather desperately. She answered Maddie's silent query with a circle of thumb and forefinger and wandered over to the window to gaze out over the beautifully manicured grounds. A pretended interest in MacGregor's handiwork might keep her from having to sit on her tender posterior and join the others in listening to a blow-by-blow description of Jessica's tennis match. She had a horrible premonition that all too soon, her poor backside would be embossed with a faithful reproduction of the tapestried dining room chairs.

The headache she had decided on as an excuse not to accompany the others was a reality by the time they had finished the coffee and Armagnac, and she signaled Maddie to wait while the others left the room. Thane had lifted his brows at her high color, but as she had done a reasonable job of disguising it with makeup, he had allowed himself to be distracted by a remark from George.

Now Maddie said, "Is that a smile or a have-a-happy-day decal? Honey, you must be in absolute agony!"

"It's a decal, and I am, and now my head's decided to get in on the act, so if you'll just mention my headache and forget the rest—I'd just as soon not advertise my attack of stupidity—I'll stay home with an aspirin and a bottle of aloe lotion."

"We'll miss you. Sure you wouldn't like me to stay here with you?"

The decal was beginning to peel off at the edges. "Thanks, Maddie, but five minutes after I'm horizontal I intend to be unconscious, so there's no use in spoiling your night out. After all, palm trees, soft music and moonlight should help the honey to flow."

Thane's expression when he challenged her decision to pass up the evening's entertainment puzzled her. It seemed comprised of equal parts of sympathy, suspicion and anger, but she was too uncomfortable to sort it out. After a brisk good-night, she detoured by the kitchen for a last check and then went to her room, making an heroic effort not to waddle as her thighs protested each step. She was caught with her caftan half off when the rap on her door came, and she allowed it to slither back into place.

It was Thane. "Would you like me to have one of the girls stay in the house with you while we're gone?"

She answered more sharply than she should have that she'd be fine if everyone would simply leave her alone! Thane's mouth tightened ominously and his changeable gray eyes sliced through her like blades of Toledo steel.

"It will be a pleasure. Perhaps you can manage at least to be civil by tomorrow."

He left her then, and she sagged against the door, feeling even more miserable, if that were possible. Darn it, she was suffering! Couldn't the man see that? Was he so blasted insensitive that he didn't know she was in pain? She had sat there at the table, pushing her food into abstract patterns while everyone else devoured Waldo's shrimp-and-ripe-olive salad, the boned and stuffed chicken leg, and the tiny buttered and dilled potatoes. She had managed a smile and a comment or two about the club tournament, and had even listened without turning green when George entertained them with a detailed description of the proper way to prepare kidneys for steak and kidney pie.

Tally had no idea what had awakened her. It couldn't have been her automatic, built-in alarm clock, for there was no sign of daylight. She lay there, gradually becoming aware of her discomfort, until the sound came again.

"Tally, are you awake?" Thane called softly from the bathroom.

"Well, if I weren't before, I am now," she grumbled, gingerly changing positions. In her sleep she had rolled over onto her back, which might account for her dreams of being carried off in the talons of a gigantic parrot. "What time is it?" she muttered, as if it were important.

"Just past midnight. Why didn't you tell me the truth?"

"What truth?" Her head was stuffed with cotton and she had fallen asleep with the lamp on, which would explain Thane's having thought she was awake.

The bathroom door opened and he strode into her room, and she struggled to sit up, barely suppressing a groan. "What do you mean, barging into my room in the middle of the night? You have no right to—"

"You have no right to give me some cooked up story about a headache when, according to Mrs. Hume, you've got third degree burns over most of your body!" He moved swiftly and silently to loom over her, his face looking dark and menacing to her sleep-befogged eyes. His thighs were pressed against the bed and all she could see was his lean, powerful muscles, barely disguised by the flawless cut of his black trousers.

"It's just a slight case of sunburn, for Lord's sake—and I *did* have a headache! And now will you please get out of here and let me go back to sleep?" It dawned on her then that her headache was gone, but her back felt as if it had been accordian-pleated and pressed with a hot iron.

A hand descended to her shoulder and she winced. Thane reached over and snapped on her bedside light, searching her face mercilessly, and this time there was no concealing makeup. "Turn over and let's see the damage," he ordered.

"Take a hike," Tally muttered inelegantly. She had foregone the wearing of a nightgown in deference to comfort, and now she clutched the sheet up under her chin.

"Tally," he warned, one hand lifting the corner of the sheet.

Panic flared in her and she grasped for a diversion. "What made you come home so early? I thought you'd be waltzing your way into sunrise."

"I called Mrs. Hume to have her send one of the girls over to check on you and she told me what you'd done to yourself today. What the devil was the point in pretending, Tally? Did you think I'd send you packing for being so stupid?"

She shrugged, and the motion was enough to cause a grimace of pain. Now that it was out in the open, she was beginning to wonder herself. It might have been stupid to fall asleep in the sun, but it was no crime. People did it every day. "I don't know," she admitted in a small voice. "I guess it was pretty foolish."

"You know it was pretty foolish." The bed lurched as it accepted his weight beside her. "There's no reason for you to try to compete with Maddie and Jess for a tan. They've spent a lifetime on the courts and the links, and besides, neither of them has your particular brand of coloring." He reached out to stroke the pale side of her face, and she was suddenly more aware of his touch than she was of the tenderness of the other side. "Don't you know how beautiful your skin is, Tally? Didn't you ever have an overwhelming compulsion to stroke a marble statue?" His fingers trailed over her cheek to circle the small, flat ear half hidden in the tumble of dark hair, and her breath was suspended somewhere between an erratic heart and a pair of softly startled lips.

Mesmerized by the rapid darkening of his eyes under lowering lids, Tally felt the sheet bind her breasts as he reached one arm across her, and then his breath fanned over her throat as he searched her face for—for what?

No time to wonder. When his mouth touched hers it was as if the air surrounding them suddenly ignited, and she was caught up into a firestorm that threatened her very sanity. The sensuous brush of his firm lips over hers sent her careening off into a flurry of half-formed rationalizations. It was insane! It was only a dream. It was only because she had been awakened in the middle of the night; with no before and after to cling to, reality was temporarily suspended.

The invasion of her mouth by his probing tongue sent quicksilver tremors coursing through her body. Her arms were pinned to her sides by the straight-jacket of the sheet and she was helpless to fight off the discovering hands that traced the lines of her hips, curved into her waist and gently stroked her stomach before mounting the small rise of her breast. His mouth abandoned her lips to seek the nerve points at the base of her throat, and then she felt the coolness of air striking her overheated body as Thane gently lowered the sheet to her waist.

"Thane, no . . . please, no," Tally whispered, her voice a flimsy thread of sound that scarcely registered against the thundering of her heart, the rasping sound of her breath—or was it his? His hungry mouth continued on its tour of her body, seeking and finding the pink velvet centers of her breasts and turning them into tiny baroque crowns. As he continued to arouse her with skillful swirls of his tongue, Tally felt the air leave her lungs in a soft whimper.

She was devastated, her defenses annihilated by an experienced assault on weaknesses she never even knew she had. She felt, rather than saw the movement when Thane sat up to remove his jacket, and she reached for him impatiently, drawing him back down to her. Her hands coursed restlessly over his shoulders, her fingers digging into the taut muscles, and when he covered her body with his, she traced the sides of his face, his ears, with an eager touch before moving on to grasp the warm vitality of his pale hair.

Gone was all sensation of pain; gone the awareness of her red, blistered back. She only knew a sweet, compulsive demand that gathered strength inside her and threatened to sweep away every vestige of common sense.

Thane reached out to snap off the bedside light and her eyes followed the movement of his hand, jealous of anything he touched that wasn't herself. Her eye fell on David's picture.

"Oh, Lord," she groaned, covering her eyes with her hands. Was she crazy? Had the sun baked her feeble brain? "Thane, please—I can't."

She felt the sudden tensing of muscles already rock hard, heard the answering stillness, and then he lifted himself from her and the sound of his soft oath cut through the tension like a sword. "Whew! Honey, you play rough!"

"Thane, I don't know what to say." It was as much her fault as his—more perhaps.

"No, but you sure as the devil know when to say it, don't you? What happened—as a matter of clinical interest?" The harsh bitterness of his voice only added to her misery, but she couldn't blame him. She hadn't exactly fought him off.

"You mean—why not?" As certain sensations receeded, others raced in to fill the void, and she became newly conscious of her tortured skin—not that she could use that as an excuse. She at least owed him honesty. "I love David. He loves me, and he trusts me. We're going to be married as soon as . . . as soon as . . ." her voice faltered. If only he'd just go!

A trick of the light brought a bleakness to Thane's averted face. "Touching—such fidelity!" And then the momentary illusion was gone, replaced by the usual look of tough self-sufficiency that so characterized the man.

"I wish you'd go," she whispered strickenly.

"I wish I'd never come," he said bitterly, tucking his shirt back into his pants. He reached down and picked up his jacket to sling it across one shoulder. "Tally . . . I don't want you to lie awake the rest of the night wondering how you're going to face me across the breakfast table tomorrow. And you're just young enough to let something like that bother you."

She eyed him balefully. She hadn't got that far in her self-recriminations yet, but he was right—it would have come. "What do you suggest, a blindfold? For your information, I usually eat in the kitchen before you're even awake."

Impatiently he ran a hand across the back of his neck. "All right, all right, I get the point. But Tally, outside of that fiancé of yours, I expect you're pretty inexperienced. Take it from someone older and wiser; it's no big deal. Near-misses are a dime a dozen in everybody's life and it didn't mean a thing—to either one of us—so forget it." His lips thinned in what passed for a smile as a hard glint reflected from his eyes. "It would have been convenient, given the sleeping arrangements, but you're too important an addition to my staff to let a little matter like this foul things up. In case I haven't mentioned it, you're doing a superb job."

And then he was gone, leaving her staring at the afterimage of a lean, broad-shouldered back and a crop of untidy sun-bleached hair.

Chapter Five

Tally was spared the embarrassment of having to face Thane across the table, where she usually joined the others for coffee. Mrs. Hume came by her room as she was dressing and insisted on anointing her back and the backs of her legs with a special preparation. By the time Tally had slipped the soft cotton knit dress over her head, the men had already adjourned to Thane's study for a quick conference before Tom and Maddie left.

Maddie was doing some last-minute ordering of fruit baskets and Tally, having her second cup of coffee, was joined by Jessica. Somehow, she had never warmed to her the way she had to the older woman.

"You're going to be visiting your parents again on the way north, I understand," she murmured by way of making polite conversation. Thane had mentioned that the Evynses had flown south and borrowed one of Jessica's father's cars to drive the rest of the way to Palm Beach.

Jessica lifted a penciled eyebrow and surveyed Tally with an openly mocking smile. "Since you're so vitally interested—yes. For a few days, at least, and then Mum and Daddy will be joining friends in Vancouver for an Alaskan cruise. Anything else?"

Tally bit her tongue. One more day—two at the most. She had run into worse in her career as a HouseSpouse; she could put up with Jessica's sweet-sour sense of humor for a few more hours.

"I understand you won your match yesterday. Congratulations." Let her make something of that! Tally focused her gaze just above and slightly to the left of the part in Jessica's frosted hair and waited for the other woman to finish her coffee. Darned if she'd turn tail and run!

"Do you play? No, I believe you mentioned you were no good at sports."

To tell the truth, Tally had flunked phys. ed. at school. Not an easy feat, but then she had never been able to see the point of directing a ball to a certain spot, only to have it knocked, kicked, or thrown somewhere else. She'd much rather be in the art studio, and her irreverent attitude toward sports had incensed the phys. ed. instructor all out of proportion.

Jessica continued, grinding out a cigarette in her saucer in spite of the fact that Tally had placed ashtrays in every room. "I can't help but wonder just where Thane ran across you. Perhaps he's baby-sitting you for your parents. Is that it—are your parents friends of his?"

Tally rose and began placing the cups and saucers

on the coffee tray. "Actually, I'm a friend of two of Thane's uncles." She refused to elaborate, in spite of Jessica's questioning look.

The silky, well-bred voice fired the parting shot from near the door. "Oh, well—I don't suppose it matters. All the same, darling, if you're hoping to attract his attention with your charming domesticity, you may as well forget it." Tally's gasp didn't go unnoticed, unfortunately. "Oh, yes, we've all had a laugh at your trying your hand at the role of Mrs. Thane Coulter. Or maybe you're just trying to pay your room and board while you're here—one way or another. Did you think that little chip of glass you're wearing on your left hand would fool anyone when we all know you're sharing Thane's suite? Well, I wish you the joy of it while it lasts, darling—but don't get your hopes up. Thane has exquisite taste in women, if I do say so myself."

Tally's hand closed tightly on the insulated handle of the silver coffeepot. It was pure spite, she told herself. A lot of nonsense from a woman who wanted to have her cake and eat it, too. She had not missed the seductive way Jessica looked at Thane, touched him every chance she had. Tally only wished she could tell the irritating creature that, far from being a contender in the Thane stakes, she was merely doing a job for a percentage of the hefty check Thane would be paying HouseSpouse, Inc. at the end of the two-week period.

One week to go, and she wished she could walk out right now and send Sybil to take her place. She really did! She felt as if she were sailing under false colors and it was not a feeling she enjoyed. What was wrong with admitting that she was hired to pinch hit for the housekeeper and serve as a one-woman entertainment committee for the visiting firemen—or their wives, at least? Was Thane afraid that his high-powered guests would turn up their aristocratic noses at being shepherded around by the hired help?

Not Maddie. Jessica, perhaps, but then Jessica had looked after herself, thank goodness. Here's hoping the Cartwrights would be more like the Taylors than like the blue-blooded, gold-plated Evynses! They couldn't even spell their name the way ordinary mortals did!

After locating Faye and having her clear away the breakfast things from the jalousied porch, Tally hurried to her room and splashed cold water on her face and wrists. When she was thirteen she had secretly wondered if her quick temper had had anything to do with her mother's running away. Of course, she had long since outgrown that childish idea. All the same, she had worked hard at learning to keep her emotions in check. Just lately, however . . .

She ran into Thane on her way to the small room she used as an office. His casual greeting restored some of her shaky composure. "Ready for the next influx of visitors? We'll have a breathing spell, at least. George tells me they'll be leaving tonight after dinner, so I hope you have another memorable meal planned."

"Lime soup, baked pompano with pasta al burro, and mandarin soufflé to follow."

"Sounds great. I must say, the meals have been a lot more imaginative since you came on the scene. Mrs. Hume and Waldo were at each other's throats, with Waldo threatening to walk out and Mrs. Hume egging him on—no pun intended." He grinned down at her. She was on her way to call about having a

Wedgewood tureen repaired; Lucy had been a little more casual than usual in putting things away last night.

"I can't imagine what a bachelor needs with a chef, anyway," she murmured, and instantly regretted turning the conversation to the personal.

"Waldo belongs to my parents. So does the whole staff, for that matter. If I'd known what a job it was going to be, running a place like this and a staff of six, I might have joined the foreign legion instead."

"I doubt it," she retorted dryly. She couldn't picture him against any other background than this —and then, oddly enough, she could. There was a toughness about Thane Coulter that would make him a survivor in any set of circumstances. A most complex man . . . a most disturbing one, too, unfortunately.

"A penny for them," he prompted, and she became aware that he had been watching her while she had tried to sort him into a nice, safe pigeonhole.

"Haven't you heard about inflation?" she snapped, smiling in spite of herself.

Ignoring her question, he said, "You enhance a background like this, Tally. Are you sure you won't grow bored with a five-room bungalow and an ever increasing number of little dependents?"

The smile disappeared instantly. "You forget, I love David. I'll love his children and I'll love whatever he can provide in the way of a home. But you couldn't possibly understand something like that."

"Couldn't I?" His head came up sharply as he bored into her with those searching eyes. "Does having a comfortable bank balance automatically preclude my having any of the normal human emotional requirements?"

She flinched from the deserved attack. The pale side of her face grew pink with the effort to bring forth an apology, but he cut her short.

"You're either an inverted snob, Tally, or incredibly narrow-minded. Probably both."

He continued to study her until her embarrassment gave way to rising temper—again. A fat lot of good it did to splash in cold water and spray on a whiff of soothing, refreshing cologne! "If that's all, Mr. Coulter, I need to make a phone call—a business call," she stressed. She hated to be put on the defensive, but darned if she'd apologize to him now. "If anyone here is a snob, Mr. Coulter, it's—"

"If you 'mister' me one more time, young lady, I'm going to see that your bottom is as red as your back, and believe me, you won't fall asleep getting this tanning!"

Her eyes flashed dangerously. Her mouth opened to tell him what he could do with his job and his contract and he closed it for her with a forefinger under her chin. "I'm not finished yet. Three more items and then you can go slam a few doors and kick something unbreakable." He held up a staying hand when her mouth opened again, and she clamped it shut, determined to hear him out before walking off the job. "Item one: no more sunbathing. I can't spare you at the moment, and one more stunt like yesterday's will land you in the hospital. Item two: use the pool anytime you want to, but not alone. If I'm not around, then get one of the girls to go in with you. No matter how competent you are, it's never a good idea to swim alone."

Grimly, she nodded, a militant sparkle in her cheeks. The fact that she had misunderstood his objections to her late-night swim only added fuel to the fires of her temper. "And item three?" she grated out.

A subtle change came down over his well-cut features. "Item three—ah, yes. Purely as a matter of curiosity, Tally, why, when you're so head over heels in love with your David, did you respond to me the way you did?"

Her head flew around and she glared at him furiously. "You might at least have the good taste not to—"

"And you did respond, Tally," he went on as if she hadn't spoken, as if she hadn't been frantically and instinctively throwing up barriers between them from the first time she had laid eyes on the man. "Even with your head pounding and your back on fire, you forgot all about it when I kissed you, and if I hadn't made the tactical error of reaching for the light, we'd have had an entirely different ending to that little episode."

She turned to escape and he caught her arm. "Don't run from me, girl! Grant me the experience to know when a woman wants me to make love to her. And you wanted it, Tally. You wanted it as much as I did, so where does that leave all your fine theories about love and happily ever after?"

"I don't want to talk about it!"

"No, I'll bet you don't," he mocked, and then his tone changed. Lifting a tendril of hair, he blew softly on her blistered nape. "But it's a fact, Tally, whether or not you're honest enough to admit it."

Her voice hoarse with embarrassment, she turned and shook his hand from her arm. "All right, so I admit you're expert enough to make a woman want you, at least temporarily, but it's only a—only a chemical reaction!"

His burst of laughter rocked her back on her heels.

"Chemistry, is it? Ah, Tally, you're priceless!" The laughter faded, leaving behind a trace of something she found impossible to interpret as he blocked her second attempt at retreat. "Honey, I may not know much about your idea of love, but don't underestimate this thing you call chemistry. It's a pretty potent force."

"Compared to love, it's nothing!" she asserted, struggling against the effect his nearness was having on her nerves.

"I'd be careful about issuing challenges if I were you, Tally." His soft words followed her as she surged through the doorway and shut the door resoundingly after her.

One more week. She couldn't do it! Even if she had to forfeit the first week's pay, she couldn't stay here and allow him to stick pins in her just for his amusement.

But what about the Cartwrights? What about her chance-in-a-million opportunity to find out where to start searching for David? She had studied everything she could lay hands on about the country and the mining industry, but there was no substitute for firsthand information. Was it worth bearing up under Thane's taunting remarks, his irritating habit of studying her with that dissecting gaze of his?

Darned right it was! She'd stick it out, if only to prove to herself that he was wrong about her—wrong about chemistry versus love!

Watching the jet thunder down the runway a few hours later, Tally felt as if her only ally were deserting her. In just one week she had grown suprisingly fond of the tall, gray-haired woman and she'd miss her. At least since that unfortunate interview with her employer, a truce of sorts seemed to be in effect. Perhaps he regretted baiting her. It was hardly fair, considering their relative positions, but after all, they were both reasonable adults, and Tally was no quitter. If they could keep their dealings on this same cool, impersonal level, then there should be no problem in getting through the following week.

Headed back on Australian Avenue after seeir the Taylors off, Thane discussed the importance of the following week. "There are at least three American companies interested. It just so happened that I met Cartwright last year out in Queensland, and I kept in touch. When I heard he was coming to this area for personal reasons, I moved fast. It's all strictly unofficial at this point, which is why I preferred to have George and Tom come here instead of my going up to the main office. When the time is right, we'll be ready to move fast."

"Talk about moving fast, I wish you'd found out whether or not I'll need to rent cribs or put up all the breakables out of reach. You would think that when a man is planning to take advantage of your hospitality, the least he could do is give out a few vital statistics."

Thane glanced at her as he pulled up for a stoplight. "Sorry—my fault. His secretary called after they'd taken off on the first leg of the flight, and it seems the children are a daughter and a new son-in-law who happens to be from this neck of the woods. Thus the trip, in the first place, I suppose."

Tally took in that information and mentally redistributed the coming guests. In the more relaxed atmosphere, she asked Thane if he'd mind going a few blocks out of the way to let her run in and see that everything was all right at home. There'd be mail, and the plants to water. She had been by twice in the past week, but she might be busy once the next houseful arrived.

"I'll only be a minute," she promised, opening the door as soon as the dark red Jaguar came to a halt at the curb. She didn't want him offering to go inside with her. It was too reminiscent of their first meeting.

"Take your time," he offered laconically, clipping the end of a cheroot. "George and Jess won't be back until about six." The Evynses were spending their last afternoon with old friends at the Swordfish Club.

The house had that closed-up smell, and she wished there was time to open the windows for a few hours. Picking up the stack of mail, she perched on the edge of Claire's zebra print sectional sofa. Circulars, mostly; junk catalogs, power bill, auto insurance—that would be a whopper. There were two personal letters for Judy, and . . .

She caught her breath as a sharp spear of pain stabbed at her. It had been over two years since she had seen that handwriting, but there was no mistaking her father's ornate capital letters. Why, after a silence of two years, was he writing now? Now that the wounds had healed over, at least superficially?

When Thane finally shoved open the door impatiently, demanding to know if she planned to spend the night, Tally was still seated on the edge of the couch, a single sheet of lined paper dangling from her fingers. On the floor was a torn envelope and not far from it lay a pink rectangle with the logo of a Tampa bank in one corner.

"Tally? What is it?"

Slowly, with a curious sort of detachment, she lifted her head and looked at the man as if she'd never seen him before. She didn't speak. There was a bewildered expression in her eyes, a bruised look that had not been there minutes before.

Firm strides brought him to her side and he removed the letter from her nerveless fingers, openly reading the two short paragraphs over the signature. When he finished, he asked her, "What does it mean?"

With a tremendous effort, Tally roused herself and took a deep breath. Her voice, when she answered him, was calm—almost gentle. "It means that my father has been writing to me all along, sending me money to go to college, only I haven't been getting the letters. It means that he didn't just go off and forget me, that he still loves me. It means the checks have been cashed, or he would have known. It means . . . it means . . ." She faltered, her eyes slowly filling with blinding tears.

Thane stepped over the heavy, expensive new coffee table and sat down, gathering her to him, and the dam broke. With no thought of the strained relations between them, with no thought at all but for the bitter sense of loss, Tally wept for all the wasted years, for all the unanswered letters her father had continued to write her. He had gone on loving her, even when it must have seemed to him that she had refused to forgive him for deserting her.

She cried angry tears for the cruelty of the woman she had credited with giving her a home, when all along Claire had been well paid for her troubles. The money didn't matter, but to have kept her father's letters from her!

With uncharacteristic patience, Thane held her until the shuddering sobs ceased. She sniffled several times, hiccoughed once, and he asked, "Better now?"

She nodded, smearing his shirtfront with tears,

and he held her away and mopped her face as if she were a child. One heavy arm was still draped over her shoulders and, in spite of the discomfort of her sunburn, she was aware of the strength to be drawn from his solid male warmth. After a few swallowed gulps, the turbulence faded and she began to consider her next step. She'd have to leave. She couldn't trust herself to be here when Claire came back from Las Vegas.

And whose money had paid her way? Whose money was she playing with even now?

The flare of anger subsided slightly when Thane demanded to know what was going on. He had read the letter from Rex Fitzsimmons asking how she was doing with her art studies; mentioning the fact that this month's check was smaller than last month's, but that the next one would make up for it; asking almost diffidently if she could find time to drop him a postcard. It took only a few minutes to give him the whole story. Nor did it occur to Tally that her muddled personal affairs were none of his business.

"We'll pack your things now and Hume can collect them later," he declared briskly after hearing a brief resume of the past few years. "Will you write to your father?" This as they were climbing the deeply carpeted stairs.

"Of course I will! If you only knew!" She laughed shakily, struggling with the mixture of relief and happiness over her father, and the anger and disgust she felt for Claire. "Of course I will, and now that I have his current address, I can call him through the marine operator! I didn't know—I tried, but he had changed ships and . . . Oh, Thane, you can't imagine how I feel!"

His smile warmed her and she ignored the shade of reserve she sensed behind the comforting warmth. Thane couldn't possibly know of the doubts that had assailed her since her father had dropped out of sight. It had been too poignant a reminder of the time her mother had left them with no warning at all, and even though Tally had tried to understand, especially as she got older and began to receive an occasional letter from her mother, sometimes she felt as if her whole life had been built on quicksand.

And then, on top of all that, David had stopped writing. It had taken a superhuman effort to convince herself she wasn't really a pariah, that people in today's transient society often lost touch with one another, it was only a temporary thing.

One by one, her sheep had come home, she mused, opening the door to the small bedroom under the eaves. Her mother had written after several months, begging Tally's understanding—she had simply not been able to handle being a sailor's wife, with long months alone. She had hoped to jolt Rex into giving up his profession, but she had met someone in Ontario and fallen desperately and unexpectedly in love, and some day Tally would understand.

"Just get what you need immediately. How much of this stuff is yours?" Thane broke into her thoughts.

"Hmmm? Oh, the furniture's all Claire's. I got my pick when she redecorated the house." And who helped pay for the poison green carpet and that tacky zebra print monstrosity downstairs? "I wouldn't let her touch this room—not that she offered," Tally laughed.

She could actually laugh about it! Recognizing the source of her spurious strength, she reached out spontaneously to touch Thane's arm. "Don't leave me—please." She was uncertain of the depth of meaning in her words, unwilling even to consider it now. She was only grateful for his presence, for his automatic assumption of control. Without it she might have started throwing things!

It didn't amount to all that much. Three boxes of odds and ends and two large suitcases. Thank goodness there were no seasonal things packed away in mothballs. Poor Hume . . . poor *Thane!* She'd have to commandeer a corner of his house until she could make other arrangements.

It was more imperative than ever that she locate David and fly out to join him. Renting cost an arm and a leg, and bunking with Sara was out of the question now. She had finally met a man, an ugly-attractive yacht broker, and Tally wouldn't want to barge in at this point in their tenuous relationship.

The next few hours rolled over her like a light fog, leaving her virtually untouched. Jessica was at her wittiest, and most of her gems were barbed. If more than a few of them were aimed at Tally, they glanced off harmlessly. She supposed the meal was a success. Faye was dispatched to help the Evynses with last-minute packing, and finally they were gone.

Thane returned from seeing them off and hooked an ottoman over closer to Tally's chair. It was almost ten o'clock and the events of the day had taken their toll, leaving her wondering if her shaky legs could carry her as far as her bedroom.

"Got yourself in hand?" His measuring eyes swept over her, lingering on the paler than usual face with the bright pink touches on one side.

She nodded, taking in another gulp of air. The deep breaths seemed to have a sort of compulsive quality to them, each one leaving her with a funny, trembly feeling at the base of her throat that warned her that another round of tears was on the way. She grabbed the arms of the chair, braced to launch herself and escape Thane's uncomfortable scrutiny.

"Time you were in bed, honey. We have the weekend before us to recuperate, and since the Cartwrights aren't due in until late Sunday, why don't we take a run outside in the *Pearl Fisher* tomorrow?"

The tears retreated and she assayed a watery smile. Absurdly enough, Thane felt like the closest thing she had to a friend at the moment, and she wasn't about to resume hostilities. "Whoever or whatever the *Pearl Fisher* is, I'd love it. I really have had better days, you know."

"I devoutly hope so. Let me fix you something tall, cool and medicinal."

He made her a mild highball and she settled back in the deep lounge chair. Sipping it, she watched the expressions flicker across his strong, attractive face as he stared absently out at the softly lit garden.

After several moments passed, Thane turned back to her. "Tally, have you considered what you're going to do after next week is up?"

Chapter Six

Doing her best to marshal her thoughts into some coherent pattern, Tally gradually readjusted her position so that, by the time she started to speak, she was sitting well forward in her chair, her feet primly side by side on the floor. Both were bare, her shoes having been slipped off earlier. Clasping her hands in her lap, she said evenly, "Well, of course, David and I will be getting married as soon as—that is, we . . ."

Thane allowed her the time she needed. He was relaxing against the down-filled cushions of the sofa, and, without turning her head, she could feel his eyes on her. It made her oddly restless.

Retrieving her drink from the end table, she downed it in three gulps and wondered how she was going to get out of telling him everything. And then she wondered why she should bother to resist. Unloading onto Thane's accommodating shoulders had felt so good once, why shouldn't she do it again? In a few days' time, she'd be walking out of here, and any secrets she divulged would no longer have any significance. Bracing herself, she said, "The only thing is—well, David and I seem to have lost contact. Temporarily. You see, he wasn't quite sure where he'd be staying after he left Allied . . . *if* he left Allied. Did I tell you he's in mining? In Australia? That's a coincidence, isn't it?"

She tried for a bright smile and felt it wobble off into space. "Yes, well—anyway, he is. Bauxite." She tried to project a picture of David's beloved features against her mind's eye and failed miserably. The only thing on her mental screen was a compelling vision of darkly tanned, strongly chiseled features, a crop of sun-bleached hair and a pair of cool gray eyes under thick, dark brows. Racing headlong into speech again, she said, "So you see, it's a good thing about the Cartwrights. I mean, Australia and mining and all. I mean, they'll know where a mining engineer might have gone after leaving Weipa. That's where David was the last time I heard from him."

When Thane continued to study her silently, her desperation grew. She could read nothing at all from his face, and suddenly she felt near to collapse. It had been too much—last night, today's departures, her father's letter and now this. It was as if just speaking about David had opened up the doubts that had crept in when her letters had come back to her stamped addressee unknown.

"You're out on your feet, honey. Why not have an early night—if it's not already too late." Thane grinned. "Tomorrow we'll head for the open sea and leave our landlocked problems behind us for a few hours."

* * *

The outing had to be postponed, however. Tally woke up to the sound of heavy rain. "I'll put in a call to Daddy," she murmured, sitting up in bed with her arms circling her updrawn knees. She had been half afraid to speak to him after all that had happened. With no conscious decision, she knew she wasn't going to make an issue of Claire's greed. The whole thing would have to come out sooner or later, but she didn't want it to mar their reunion.

Even her call had to be postponed, though, when she discovered that Faye had come down with a virus of some sort. Mrs. Hume was up and about, walking as if she had a bowl of water balanced on her head, and Tally encouraged her to leave everything to Tally and Lucy. The two of them could manage just fine, especially as the rooms had been freshly made up and the meals were already planned through Tuesday.

At eleven she managed to escape for a minute and she hurried to the library, which Thane used as a home office. He was there, seated at his desk, and he looked up apologetically as she barged in.

"I thought as long as we had to postpone our trip I'd handle a few things in here. It'll be clear by tomorrow—I guarantee it."

"Thane, could I place a ship-to-shore call?" she asked.

"How about a shore-to-ship call? I'll get the marine operator for you and leave you to it, all right?" He put down an empty coffee cup and reached for the phone, but before he could do more, Lucy stuck her head through the door and said, "Tally, you have a—"

"Tally! So this is where you've gotten to!" Judy

exclaimed, ignoring the maid and gliding through the open door.

The next few minutes were taken up with introductions. Judy settled herself into the green Chinese pheasant chair, arranging her long, tanned limbs for maximum exposure in the slit white sharkskin skirt. She looked more beautiful than ever, all five feet nine inches of her groomed to perfection. As a model, even if only part-time, Judy knew how to make the most of very good material.

"When did you get back?" Tally asked, subsiding into the chair against the wall. She had no idea whether or not Judy knew about the checks and the letters. She didn't want to know.

The tall blonde took her time in answering. She was happily evaluating everything in the room, including Thane, Tally noted with surprising displeasure. "Oh, I got back yesterday. Mother stayed on in Vegas. She's *met* someone, if you know what I mean." The implication was clear, but Tally ignored it. She didn't want to think about Claire now. "I missed you. I called Sara and she told me where you were working. Aren't you lucky!"

Judy accepted a cigarette from Thane and leaned back again to expel a graceful stream of smoke. "And aren't I *un*lucky," she murmured with a small moue. "You know how I abhor staying home alone." She managed a rather overdone sigh, which incidentally caused considerable upheaval in the area where her shirt button met across her generous bosom. "But I don't suppose I could ask you to give up all this just to save me from getting a bad case of the willy-wobbles."

They were interrupted when Lucy brought in a tray of coffee, her eyes glistening with curiosity as she placed it on the desk. By the time Tally had poured and served, Judy was regaling Thane with a list of possible mutual acquaintances. Tally subsided with her own cup of Waldo's perfectly brewed coffee and studied her stepsister.

The vacation had certainly done her good. When Tally had driven them both to the airport, Judy had been pale and drawn looking, not an easy feat for a tall, tanned blonde with peach-toned cheeks and, thanks to a pair of tinted contacts, glittering turquoise eyes. She was certainly fully recovered now, and Thane was getting the full benefit of all two hundred and twenty volts.

"I've seen you around the Swordfish Club," Judy confided, leaning her elbows on the desk and using that little trick she had demonstrated to Tally years ago of widening her eyes just a fraction to punctuate her words.

Tally was amused at her blatant tactics. At least she thought it was amusement she was feeling. Maybe she'd better not hang around to find out. "I'd better go see about lunch."

"Judy, you'll stay, of course." That was Thane, his eyes obviously appreciating the self-guided tour of Judy's stellar attractions.

"Thanks, Thane, I'd love to!"

Thane! Judy! Five minutes after meeting they were on a first name basis, dragging up all sorts of farfetched connections as if they'd known each other all their lives! Just because Judy was a West Palm native and Tally had grown up in Otter Creek!

By the time they had finished Waldo's asparagus soup and shrimp salad, Thane and Judy were comparing notes on last month's regatta. Judy had attended with the boyfriend of the moment, a middle-aged insurance tycoon. Tally excused herself and hurried out to the kitchen. She untangled Lucy and Waldo after the maid's refusal to shuck clams, and suggested Waldo stick them in the freezer for a few hours to make the onerous chore easier. Sometimes she agreed with the housekeeper; a plain old cook would be easier to work with than a temperamental chef with an exaggerated notion of his own dignity.

By the time she rejoined Thane and Judy in the East Room, it was all settled. Judy met her at the door. "Oh, darling, guess what! Thane's invited me to stay here until I go back to school on Monday week. Isn't that super?"

No! It was a lot of things, to Tally's way of thinking, and super was not among them. She was used to Judy's manipulating people to get whatever she wanted, but somehow, she hadn't expected Thane to be quite such a pushover—or maybe he hadn't minded. "I thought Claire was coming back in a day or so."

"Oh, well, she may—then again, she may not. Mother's a big girl now, and after all, there's certainly nothing left of her relationship with Rex. Even you'll have to admit that."

Tally's lips tightened and she flicked a glance toward the library door where Thane had disappeared. She'd hide her dismay if it killed her! For years she had sought a closer relationship with her stepsister, and now, when Judy was making the effort for a change, she wished she'd never bothered. Which doesn't cast me in a very charitable light, Tally admitted with chagrin. "You'll want to run home and pack a few things," she murmured.

"Oh, they're in the car. I thought I might check into a hotel until Mother got back," Judy replied airily.

I'll just bet you did, Tally thought. Aloud, she said, "I'll have Hume bring them inside. I guess you can share my room, since the guest rooms are all ready for the next batch of company."

Judy professed herself thrilled with everything, and it didn't take her long to discover the relationship between Thane's room and Tally's when she went to the bathroom to remove her blue-green contacts. Her eyes widened in amusement. "We-lll, aren't you the clever little thing? But darling, don't you know you can't promote anything really interesting as long as you keep poor old David's photo beside your bed?"

Irritably, Tally shoved her dresses aside to make room for Judy's things in the closet. "Don't be ridiculous," she muttered. "What should I do, bunk in with the guests, or shove the Humes over in their apartment? They already have Faye and Lucy with them. Here, you can have the top two drawers, too."

But Judy's gaze still lingered on the contents of the closet. She reached out and allowed the fern printed chiffon to flow over her fingers. "Have I missed out on something lately? Did you decide to blow your savings on these things and hitchhike to Australia?"

Reluctantly, Tally explained, having to elaborate far more than she wished before she felt she had justified her acceptance of several hundred dollars' worth of clothing.

"Hmmmm." Judy's blue-gray eyes narrowed speculatively. "You know, love, I feel an attack of sisterly devotion coming on. I'm going to help you with your job. In fact, I'm going to have a ball helping you with your job!" She smiled contentedly and examined her reflection in the mirror.

They dined at the club, as Waldo had been promised the evening off. The rain had stopped by late afternoon, and Tally gazed longingly at the slacks and shirt she had planned to wear on Thane's boat. Instead she reached for a simply cut dinner suit of pale aquamarine. It made her eyes look almost purple, and with makeup, she was able to disguise her lingering sunburn successfully. Judy managed to tie up the bathroom for hours, reminding Tally of Thane's opinion on that matter. She finally emerged, her eyes glittering with the tinted contacts and her makeup applied with a masterful hand. By the time the two of them left the bedroom together, Tally felt totally eclipsed by her tall, stunning stepsister in the diamanté-trimmed, peacock blue silk.

To make matters worse, her feet hurt. She kept forgetting to buy herself another pair of evening shoes until she needed them, and then it was too late.

The meal must have been good. Thane certainly seemed to enjoy his, and Judy did justice to her broiled fish and salad. Tally might as well have dined on her linen napkin for all the enjoyment she got out of it. But when the dessert cart was wheeled around and Judy shuddered delicately, Tally took perverse delight in ordering a slice of amaretto torte. She was almost ill by the time she had devoured the last morsel.

Tally excused herself to go to the ladies' room after dinner. By the time she returned, Thane and

Judy had been joined by a mutual acquaintance. When the dancing started, Judy quickly claimed Thane, leaving Tally to listen to Monte Wirther's account of his latest real estate coup.

Her eyes must have glazed over. The stocky, self-important businessman came to a reluctant halt in his monolog and asked her to dance. Tally decided she'd rather dance with the man than embarrass him and disgrace herself by falling asleep at the table, but she had forgotten the condition of her sandals. By the time she had limped through two consecutive numbers, she was ready to surrender. She refused the next dance, using tiredness as an excuse, and was chagrined when Thane appeared beside the table, holding his hand out to her. She had no choice but to refuse, nor did she miss the tightening of his lips. Evidently he wasn't used to being turned down. The thought gave her small satisfaction.

Tally had gone easy on the wine at dinner, but now she felt parched. It was terribly warm in the crowded room in spite of jalousied windows that looked out over the water. Thane eyed her narrowly, but then Judy appeared at his side with still another mutual friend, and Tally felt as if she had somehow faded into the woodwork. She simply hadn't the energy to do more than acknowledge the introductions.

The music started again and once more Thane held out a hand to her. Tempted, Tally's discomfort won out. By now her throat was sore from trying to talk over the din, and her head was swimming. Someone had refilled the glasses and she must have drunk hers down without even noticing. It was so hot in here!

When Judy invited Thane out onto the dance floor

again, Tally made up her mind. She simply couldn't stick it out any longer. "Monte, would you mind terribly driving me home? To tell the truth, I'm not used to late nights and my head's beginning to rebel."

She felt guilty for her dislike of the rather pompous man when he immediately rose to his feet, all sympathy and solicitude. He signed for their drinks and ordered his car brought around. It was while they were waiting that Tally's eyes sought Thane, only to discover him on the other side of the dimly lit room, glowering at her over Judy's shoulder as they danced.

Monte was blessedly silent on the short drive home. Tally struggled with an aching head and an overdose of self-pity. Thane could have asked her to dance first, before the soles of her feet had become so tender from the worn-out soles of those blasted sandals! And he didn't have to devote every single minute to Judy, no matter how many friends they had in common.

If she was being slightly unfair, considering that Judy had done most of the running, she was in no condition to recognize that fact. By the time Monte pulled up in front of the house, she had decided that Thane would make an abominable brother-in-law. Stepbrother-in-law. Whatever!

Padding silently through the empty house, Tally felt like dissolving into tears for no other reason than that her feet hurt, her head hurt, and her heart hurt. Which was ridiculous!

Besides all that, her throat was beginning to protest an evening spent in a smoky atmosphere. She scrambled around in Thane's medicine cabinet and found the aspirin. She wanted to be fast asleep by the time Judy crept in because she had no intention of listening to a blow-by-blow description of her triumphant evening. Forgetting her usual good-night to David's picture, she was in bed and asleep almost before her body had warmed the linen sheets.

Chapter Seven

The linen was more than warm by the time Tally opened her eyes again. Sometime during the night she had kicked off the top sheet, and when she blinked painfully awake to the sight of Judy's unmade bed a few feet away, she was aware of several things at once.

Her skin hurt, almost as much as it had when she had burned herself, but this time she hurt all over. Her throat was raw and she was parched dry, but overriding all this was the unfocused misery that had to do with Judy's being there, with Thane and the way he had seemingly fallen for her, and with the fact that David no longer had the power to draw Tally's thoughts away from the lean, tough man with the blond hair and the threatening eyebrows.

Faye peeped around the door. "Morning, Tally. I'm back in action, so you don't have to worry about oversleeping."

"Did I oversleep?" Tally croaked, her voice hardly more than a painful rasp.

"Oh-oh. Looks like you've got what I had," Faye condoled, venturing farther into the room. "If it's any comfort to you, it doesn't last all that long, but it's purely rotten while it lasts. Mrs. Hume says your sister's staying with us. That must be her having breakfast with Mr. Thane. Boy, she's something else!"

Tally was in no mood to hear anyone's praises sung, particularly Judy's. "Did the doctor say you were contagious when you had it?" she whispered, wincing as each word was ripped from her raw throat.

"You caught it, didn't you? But don't worry, at least I can look after you. I'm immune."

Next Tally was subjected to a visit from her stepsister. Judy was furious with her and insisted that she move to another room before she spread her germs, but Thane vetoed the idea immediately. It was Judy who moved, when a two-room apartment over the gardening shed that Tally hadn't even known about was cleared for her use.

"If I come down with your bug and miss out on my next modeling assignment, Tally Fitzsimmons, I'll wring your neck!" Judy warned as she gathered up her scattered clothing. After only one day in the Coulter household, Judy had managed to make the room look as if she had lived in it for weeks. "I'm supposed to go on location at Bimini for three days next week, and if the stills look good, I've got a good shot at a long-term TV contract for Leone's. They're coming out with a whole new line of cosmetics next year, and Syd says I'm a cinch for it." She paused to study her flawless complexion in the mirror, and Tally, watching through fevered eyes, had to agree that her looks would sell any line of cosmetics.

Tally muttered something to the effect that Syd should know, Syd being Judy's agent, whom Judy alternately adored and despised, depending on which assignments she landed and which she missed out on.

"On the other hand, maybe I'll give up modeling altogether," the blonde murmured to her satisfied reflection. "Thane's got everything I've ever wanted in a man and then some. In fact, why not go for broke? A little social clout never hurt a product. Lots of debutantes have modeled."

"You're no deb," Tally croaked flatly.

"Maybe not, but Mrs. Thane Coulter of Coulter International wouldn't have any problems launching a top line of cosmetics."

"The problem might just be Thane. Somehow I can't see him allowing his wife to cash in on his name."

"You just leave Thane to me, darling," Judy purred, scooping up several pairs of panty hose and stuffing them into her suitcase. "If I've left anything, send Whatsername over with it, will you? I'm liking this apartment idea more and more all the time. Privacy, you know," she said with a glittery smile over her shoulder as she placed her bags outside the door for Hume to collect.

It was Sunday. The Cartwrights were due in today and Tally was too miserable to care. She saw nothing more of Judy, and indeed, the whole staff seemed too busy to do much more than glance in occasionally during the day. Mrs. Hume had dosed her after a breakfast which she left untouched, and she came in again with a lunch tray, shaking her gray head disapprovingly at Judy's unmade bed.

"Fat lot o' good that one will be, can't even spread her own bed. My girls have better things to do than look after the likes of her, begging your pardon, Miss Tally. Here—you're going to taste this, at least. Waldo made it specially for you." She spooned up some of the clear broth and Tally leaned up on one elbow to sip from the bowl of the spoon.

"It's delicious," she whispered hoarsely, "but I'm really not hungry. If I could just have something else to drink?"

She had fruit juice with the medicine the doctor had left her and fell back into a restless sleep. When next she opened her eyes it was to see Thane sitting on the foot of her bed. It had been the impression of something touching her leg that had awakened her, and when she opened her eyes more fully she saw that he was tracing the outline of her leg through the dark green silk spread.

Seeing her eyes open, he said, "Poor baby, I didn't do you any favors when I brought you into my home, did I?"

"A little gainful employment never hurt anyone," Tally replied huskily. She attempted a smile and it felt as if her lips were cracking.

"Wait a minute," Thane ordered, striding into the bathroom.

As if I planned to take off the minute his back was turned, Tally thought with uncharacteristic irritability. She could hear him clattering about in the medicine cabinet, and then he returned with a small pot of ointment.

He dipped a finger into it. "Pucker up," he ordered, anointing her dry lips with something cool and soothing. "Works wonders for windburn. Let's see how it does for fever dryness." His fingers moved caressingly over her mouth. "Better?"

She nodded and surprisingly enough, her head didn't fall off. The day's dozing seemed to have helped. "What time is it?" she managed in a slightly stronger voice.

"Quarter to six. I'm getting ready to go collect the Cartwrights in a few minutes. Your sister's offered to help entertain them for me, so you just take it easy and concentrate on getting well. The Humes are spending more time worrying about you than they are tending to their duties." He grinned, the clear gray eyes that she found so exasperatingly unreadable moving from her touseled hair to her flushed face, and down to the low rounded neckline of her rumpled batiste nightgown. "Even Waldo seems to be on his best behavior. There hasn't been an ultimatum in several hours."

"We planned shrimp creole tonight. Hudgins had some of those little brown North Carolina shrimp," Tally told him anxiously. As if the kitchen couldn't function without her.

"Look, we'll send out for chicken if it comes to that. Just stop worrying—and that's an order." He rose and moved toward the door and Tally fought down the irrational sense of loss that assailed her.

Large chunks of time disappeared. The rest were filled with pills, naps, and gallons of broth and fruit juices. Faye popped in frequently the second day, and Mrs. Hume seemed to be getting around almost normally. Tally recalled waking once to see Judy standing over her bed with an air of oddly suppressed excitement. What had that been all about? Something about a surprise, but before she could say more, Thane had come in and hustled her out—afraid of her catching the bug, no doubt.

Tally dreamed that he had returned; she roused to feel a cool, hard hand trail over her cheek to cup her chin, but when she tried to reach out to hold it to her, it was like swimming through molasses. Unable to overcome the strange inertia, she drifted back into a confused dream world.

The next time she awoke she was aware of three things in rapid succession: she was starved, her head no longer ached, and her throat was back to normal. After staring at the ceiling for several minutes while she gathered her determination, she sat up and waited for the room to stop rocking. She slid her feet to the floor and then cautiously made her way to the bathroom.

She had finished with her shower and was tucking the towel around her hair when the door burst open and Thane stood there, glowering as furiously as if he had caught her with her hand in the till.

"Would you mind telling me just what in the devil you think you're doing?" he demanded harshly.

At that particular moment, what she was doing was clutching at the silk shower curtain, partly for concealment, partly for support. By the time she had gathered her wits sufficiently to light into him for bursting in on her, he had grabbed his own navy terrycloth robe and was obviously intent on smothering her with it.

"Darn it—let me go!"

He held her with one arm and tried to force her fist through the sleeve, but her damp body defeated him and he swore softly and gathered her up in his arms, the robe dangling by one sleeve as he carried her into her room. "Who gave you permission to get out of bed?"

"Who gave you permission to invade my privacy?" she snapped back.

"I'll invade more than your privacy if you don't have any better sense than to pull a fool stunt like that! You could have fallen and broken your neck and no one would have been the wiser!"

He dumped her on her bed and neither of them seemed to notice that Tally was wet and naked. The heavy bathrobe trailed across the bed as Thane glared down at her, his fists bracing his hips as if to restrain himself from taking more direct action.

"Well . . ." Tally growled, more intimidated than she cared to reveal. "I didn't." She was frowning at the wetness that darkened the front of his shirt and then her eyes slowly lifted to his face. What she saw there made her reach hurriedly for the robe and pull it over her.

"Get dressed and I'll go get your lunch," Thane ordered tersely, both his eyes and his voice oddly flat. He snatched up the nightgown she had removed before her shower and threw it at her and she shook her head.

"Not that one. I want a fresh one—third drawer down."

He grabbed the first one he came to in her lingerie drawer and dropped it on the bed as if it burned his fingers. "Lunch," he muttered and disappeared through the door.

She was more or less composed by the time he returned with soup, crackers, and tea that was mostly milk. She had rediscovered that she was starving, and not even the sight of Thane's coiled spring form braced against her dresser was enough to slow her down.

"Don't inhale it," he jeered, and she glanced up quickly and then grinned. She felt immensely better.

"Sorry. I had to make up for lost time. Could I have more soup?"

"Better take it easy at first. I'll see what Mrs. Hume says."

She placed the tray carefully on her bedside table after moving David's picture back to make room. She wished he'd leave and, irrationally, she wanted him to stay. Must be the aftereffects of the twenty-four-hour siege. The look she sent him was almost shy. "You lucked out on your deal with House-Spouse. Has Judy been helping out in my place?"

"As it turns out, I don't have to worry about a guide for the wife and daughter." He stared in fascination at the tip of his shoe, as if the tan ostrich leather held the secrets of the universe. "It seems that the son-in-law lived in West Palm for several years."

"Oh, good—he probably has family here, then. But in that case, they'd be staying there. Or maybe they don't have room?" She was chattering. It was as if she sensed something in the atmosphere, some disturbing new element that had invaded the quiet luxury of her bedroom.

"Tally . . . damn it, there's just no easy way to tell you this!" Thane shifted his weight and Tally's unease coalesced into a cold, hard knot inside her. "The fact of the matter is, Cartwright's son-in-law is . . . someone you know."

His eyes slanted toward the photograph and Tally whispered, "David."

Dropping down beside her, Thane took her unresisting hand in his, rubbing a thumb over her knuckles while he searched her stunned expression. "Tally? Tally, listen to me." She failed to respond and he shook her hand impatiently. Her empty gaze wandered back to his face from wherever it had been. "Tally, they're not here. I met them at the airport and told them that we'd had a slight epidemic here and I booked them into the Breakers. It was later on, when I mentioned Debbie and David Loggins to your sister that she told me who he was." His eyes looked as if they would have cried for her if they could have, and she unconsciously pressed his hand. "You had never mentioned his last name," he finished helplessly.

"David," Tally murmured, her head tilted in a waiting attitude. The pain would strike her any minute now; so far, she just felt numb.

"Look, I've come up with an idea, but I thought I'd better check it out with you first."

Tally felt a growing sense of remoteness, as if none of this touched her at all. Thane was here, big and hard and solid. He had been angry with her only moments before, and she could have kicked him for his high-handedness, but none of that mattered—he was real. David was . . .

David was married to someone named Debbie. He wasn't struggling to get established out in Australia so he could send for her. He wasn't counting the days until he could add a wedding band to the small engagement ring he had placed on her finger. And it was all so unreal . . . almost funny!

Her face slowly crumpled and she pitched forward into Thane's waiting arms, burying her face in his throat as the sobs wracked her.

Gradually she became aware that Thane was rubbing her wet head with the towel that had slipped askew. One arm was holding her to his chest while he squeezed the moisture from the long ebony trendrils that were plastered to her face. "All this s-seems horribly familiar," she choked between sniffles. "I k-keep blubbering all over your poor shirts. Send the laundry bill to me, huh?"

"You do tend to get a bit soggy, but you're entitled. I don't believe I've ever met a walking soap opera before."

A sound escaped her that was somewhere between a chortle and a sob. "You know, I never managed to call Daddy."

"I did."

Her face lifted from his chest and she stared at him, noting almost absently that the lines that scored his lean cheeks seemed deeper than they had the first time she had seen him. The pared-down toughness that was so at odds with his careless urbanity seemed more pronounced than ever. "You did what?" she challenged.

"I got in touch with your father. He's on a tanker just leaving Costa Rica about now. I told him what had happened." At the sudden ignition of anger in her wet eyes, he shook her slightly. "Look, Tally, the man's not a fool. Once he knew you hadn't been getting his letters, the rest was easy to figure out. The checks had been endorsed, after all—not that either one of us mentioned the word forgery. The important thing, as far as he was concerned, was that his daughter had not stopped caring for him."

They were both silent while Tally digested the news, and then she took a steadying breath and asked, "Did you tell him I'd call? Does he know I've moved out?" Suddenly something else struck her; she had moved out with the idea that she'd soon be leaving for Australia. Now what? Use the money she had been saving to establish herself somewhere else? Why not?

"I told him the whole works, honey. About young

Loggins, too." At her protest he went on to say that Rex had asked if she was married now. She had been going steady with David the last time Rex had been home, and her letters had been full of their plans until he had changed ships and stopped writing. Or at least, she thought he had stopped writing.

Thane was speaking and her attention was jerked back by his words. "I told him we were engaged, and he'll be coming into Tampa in about a week and a half. I promised we'd meet him there."

"You wha-a-at?"

When she shoved herself away to glare up at him he brought her forcefully back against his chest. "Look, honey—"

"Don't you 'look honey' me! Thane, I'm in enough trouble as it is without you complicating matters!"

"I rather thought I was making things easier for you," he retorted witheringly.

"I'd like to know how the devil you figure that!"

"Unless you want to go weeping and wailing to that wet-behind-the-ears opportunist—"

"If you mean David, then say so!"

"All right, I'll say so! If you're addicted to martyrdom, then go throw yourself under the nearest train! The Cartwright clan will appreciate a real, live melodrama staged for their benefit, with my houseguest playing the female lead!"

"I'm not your houseguest!"

"Then what the devil are you?" His fingers were biting into her shoulders now, his eyes blazing like hot ice.

"I'm your . . . I'm not your *anything!* I'm—I'm . . ."

The fingers eased from crippling to merely punishing, and he searched her averted face. "Tally, listen to me. I don't have to tell you how important this deal is to me—and it's still on mighty shaky ground. A hint of something between you and Loggins would be all it'd take to spook Cartwright, and we'd be back to ground zero." She was drawn in spite of herself to those compelling eyes of his. "As I see it, you have two choices. You can wallow in righteous self-pity and watch Loggins squirm, or you can jump the gun and let me introduce you to the whole family as my fiancée."

"You forgot a third choice," she reminded him bitterly. "I could simply walk out and let Sara send you someone else to finish out my contract."

A sudden freeze eradicated all trace of the slight thaw in his narrowed gaze. "And you forgot that your name is on that contract. If you walk out before the two weeks is up, I can sew your friend Sara up in so much red tape she won't be able to sign her name to a grocery list," Thane said softly.

"But that's absurd! Those contracts are meant to protect us more than the client! They don't mean—"

"They mean precisely what I interpret them to mean, Tally. It's a flimsy contract, and it's got enough loopholes in it so that a smart lawyer can hang any one of the three of us with it—you, me, or Sara Drummond. And I'll be paying the lawyer to see things my way."

"You're totally heartless, aren't you?" she seethed impotently. She had finally wrenched herself away from him, and now she sat cross-legged, glaring at the navy blue terrycloth robe flung across the foot of her bed.

He hesitated before replying. "I guess I am. Maybe I'm just thinking of my own interests in this matter, but I insist we do it my way, Tally. Do I have your cooperation or do I start applying a little gentle pressure where it will do the most good?"

She gazed at him in frustrated anger. If only she didn't feel so weak from this twenty-four-hour bug! If only Thane weren't so anxious to smooth the way with the Cartwrights for his stupid company! If only Sara had given Janice this plum instead.

And in that case, Tally would probably still be hoarding pennies to fly out to meet David! Her eyes were beginning to gleam with determination when she turned to where Thane sat, seemingly relaxed while he waited for her answer. "What about Judy? She knows the whole story, and I don't think we can count on her not to blow it."

"Leave Judy to me. I'll tell her as much of the truth as she needs to know."

"Well, it'll have to be a pretty wild story, but if you think you can pull it off, I guess I'm game."

Those translucent gray eyes became as opaque as polished silver in an instant and he smiled at her. "Good. It'll be simplest all around. I'll have a selection of rings sent out immediately.

Tally's right hand covered her naked left one. David's ring was still in her dresser drawer. For some reason, she had never gotten in the habit of wearing it to bed. "That won't be necessary, surely. I mean, it's just for a week."

"But it's got to be convincing. The ring will help—and so will this." He reached for her, catching her off guard, and she toppled against him. Just before his mouth came down on her startled lips, he murmured something about rehearsals.

It took all of ten seconds for Thane to overcome her indignant reaction. Telling herself frantically that it was only because she was still weak from her recent illness, Tally felt herself opening to the probing invasion of his kiss. Her hands clutched at his arms, halfheartedly pushing him away, and then traitorously slid over his shoulders to meet behind his back. The tentative exploration swiftly took on all the earmarks of a full-fledged assault, and when he drew away, even Thane seemed shaken by the intensity of emotion that had flared briefly between them.

"I think we might need a few more practice sessions before we can pull that off with the ease of old hands," he muttered huskily.

"Did you forget I was contagious? You're going to be flat on your back in a few days unless your resistance is awfully high." Her voice was none too steady and she avoided meeting his eyes.

"Honey, I've known all along you were contagious. And as for my resistance, it's highly selective. Time will tell," he murmured, easing her down on the pillow as he stood to go. "I'll go start a few wheels rolling. See you later."

Chapter Eight

By the time they were all seated around the dinner table the following night, Tally felt as if she had wandered onstage during an avant garde play. She turned from one actor to another, hearing lines about reduction ratios and skirt lengths, production schedules and creaseproof eye shadow, and her eyes kept straying to the head of the table where Thane relaxed, nursing his wineglass as he listened to something Ed Cartwright was saying.

It was ridiculous for any man to be so attractive! He wore his dinner jacket as easily as another man might wear jeans and a T-shirt, and his striking coloring, his strongly defined features, should have been given to a . . . a male model, or a Hollywood idol!

One finger strayed to her throat. He certainly spared no expense in an effort to pull off this whole ridiculous masquerade, too. Earlier today he had grown impatient with her inability to choose a ring from the tray that had been sent out. They had all been absurdly impressive and, she was quite certain, absurdly expensive. He had finally selected a deep-toned sapphire surrounded by baguette diamonds. It had been later on, when she was dressing for her first meal in the dining room since her illness, that he had rapped on her door and entered at her bidding.

"I thought these trinkets might make a convincing engagement gift." The trinkets had been a sapphire pendant and small hoop earrings of alternating diamonds and sapphires.

"Thane, this is ridiculous! You don't need to go to these lengths just to convince David I'm not withering on the vine because of his defection."

He shrugged, tossing the leather cases onto her bed. "He'll be convinced because it's an easy out for his conscience. Cartwright isn't so gullible. I don't want him to be distracted by any untidy details in my personal life, and as for your sister . . ."

"My stepsister," Tally reminded him irritably. She felt less and less sisterly toward Judy, and she was finally convinced that the feeling was entirely mutual.

As if the mention of her name had worked a spell, the door opened and Judy swirled in with an unconvincing little gasp of surprise. "Oh—Thane. I didn't know you were in here. Am I interrupting something?" The turquoise contacts gave her eyes a strangely glittering look.

Urbane mask once more in place, Thane lifted the sapphire pendant from its flat case and turned to fasten it around Tally's neck. "I just stopped by to help Tally with the safety gadget on this thing. Can you manage the earrings, sweetheart?"

Tally could have clubbed him! She would have

given the whole show away right then and there had it not been for the priceless mixture of expressions on Judy's beautiful face. Following Tally's glance, Thane turned and blandly complimented Judy on her choice of dress. It was a sequined coral crêpe, cut down as low as possible and up as high as possible, and it struck Tally as a bit much for a quiet dinner at home.

"I'd be happy wearing a flour sack if I had something like that to spark it up with," Judy purred, her eyes crawling all over the diamond and sapphire ensemble.

Tally, disgusted with the whole pretense and strangely resentful of the way Thane's eyes followed the neckline of the sequined coral gown, said shortly, "Have you left the guests wandering around on their own?" The Cartwrights and Logginses had moved in this morning, Thane having decided the danger was over.

"David's in the East Room. I gave him a drink—he looked as if he could use a stiff one." The tall blonde looked archly at Tally. "Maybe you and your ex can slip away for a little rendezvous after dinner. Shall I keep the little bride occupied?"

Thane muttered something under his breath and Tally cast Judy a speaking look. All right, so it had been too much to hope she'd be fooled. But things were awkward enough without her mischief-making propensities!

That had been earlier. So far, Tally had not found a single minute to speak to David, even if she had wanted to. Thane had managed the reunion with surprising smoothness. "I understand you and my fiancée were friends while you lived in this area,

Loggins. Let us be among the first here in the States to congratulate you on your marriage."

David's expression had defied analysis, and then Tally had been swept up in a flurry of introductions and arrangements and she had not seen the guests again until they met for drinks before dinner.

She sat like a spectator at a tennis match during the interminable meal, while Thane and Ed Cartwright discussed the latest developments in their field, and Pam Cartwright, a ruddy-faced woman with an engaging smile, pumped Judy for all the best shops in the immediate area. David rearranged his food on his plate, looking more and more morose as the evening wore on, and his absurdly young wife sat in silent misery that brought out an unexpected protective streak in Tally.

Eventually, they made their way back into the East Room, and Tally found herself answering Debbie's questions about one of the Australian rock groups that had been a big hit in the States. Her eyes instinctively sought out Thane's commanding figure to find him engaged in a low-voiced conversation with Judy over near the drinks cabinet. She jerked her attention back to the young girl beside her.

"Your sister's terribly beautiful, isn't she?" Debbie Loggins said wistfully.

"Yes, she is." Debbie was blonde, too; but whereas Judy's coloring was vivid and highly polished, Debbie seemed to be all flyaway white hair, pink peeling skin, and long-limbed, coltish awkwardness. Tally found herself wondering just why David had married her, and then, on the heels of that, wondering why she wasn't writhing in agony. Amazingly enough, her only feeling at the moment was a vague sort of sympathy for this earnest young creature who couldn't be more than a few years younger than Tally's own twenty-two years.

As the small group migrated toward a cozy arrangement of sofas and chairs, the talk became general, and Tally leaned back and allowed it to wash over her in meaningless waves. Comparisons between the game fishing of Queensland's Barrier Islands and the Florida Keys were interspersed with ". . . really good blouse and a long skirt . . ." and ". . . complete facial—takes hours, but just this once . . ."

Tally found her attention drawn to the couple on the opposite sofa. Judy had more or less pushed Thane down and taken her place beside him, and Tally looked on with a feeling almost of nausea. Must she be so obvious about it? Thane must have let her in on the charade they were playing out, but unless she turned her voltage down when she gazed at him with those slumbrous, greedy eyes of hers, they were going to blow the whole thing.

For her own amusement, Judy was more than capable of doing just that, Tally realized with a sinking feeling, but if she had plans of her own where Thane was concerned—and it was more and more obvious that she did—then she'd better dim her light for the time being!

Perhaps it was an effort to counteract any inaccurate impression Judy might have given the Cartwrights that made Thane come up with a suggestion in the middle of the week. Judy had just announced her reluctant departure for the three-day stint in Bimini, and David was planning to spend a day with his new relatives, driving upstate to the small retirement village where his grandparents lived.

"Then Tally and I are going to make good on a

rain check," Thane told the others. His arm dropped around her shoulder as if from long habit, and she felt momentarily dizzy from the potent aura of rich tobacco and the subtle sandalwood aftershave he used. "We got rained out the last time we planned to spend a day aboard the boat, so if no one minds . . . ?"

Judy minded. Tally almost looked to see if there were holes in her blouse where a pair of turquoise lasers had burned through.

The visitors left early the next morning in a car Thane kept for the use of the staff, and an hour later, a tight-lipped Judy roared off in her yellow TR-9, taking one small bag and leaving the rest of her clothes in the apartment she seemed to have settled into permanently.

Permanently until I leave, Tally thought rancorously. Then she'll be back in the room adjoining Thane's—or will they even need more than the one?

She dressed in white jeans and a blue denim work shirt that had faded until it matched her eyes—not that she even noticed that fact. At Thane's suggestion, she stuck her yellow maillot in her purse and threw in a tube of sunscreen as an afterthought. The last of her burn was almost a memory now, and she didn't intend to repeat that performance. She was beginning to feel like Job. What was it Thane had called her? A walking soap opera? Well, a few more days and she could walk right off the stage—and the sooner the better. She was beginning to suspect a whole new play was about to be introduced, with Judy in the starring role, and she didn't want to see how it ended.

They followed Lake Drive, and Thane pulled in at the Brazilian Docks. He handed her a small straw hamper and carried the insulated chest on his shoulder, grinning down at her as if they were a couple of school kids playing hooky.

And she grinned right back. Something told her she was going to regret this day for a long, long time, but she was just fool enough to ignore the warning. After years of being practical, of filling her days and nights with working and dreaming, she was going to live for the present, and if she suffered for it later, then she could handle that, too. She was no novice when it came to suffering.

The *Pearl Fisher* was one of the more modest cruisers in the marina. Tally suspected it was not that Thane couldn't afford one of the larger ones so much as that he hadn't the time to devote to it. She had come to realize that for all his wealth, Thane had a practical streak, too. Ostentation was not among his vices.

Despite its modest size, nothing had been spared in fitting out Thane's thirty footer. She could accommodate five, and boasted air conditioning, electric appliances and a roomy head and shower. There was a wealth of mysterious looking navigational aids lined up on the oiled wood console, as well as an excellent sound system for the selection of tapes she found in one of the wall lockers.

She unpacked and put away the chilled lobster salad, the fruit, and the anchovy spread and ripe Camembert to go on the crisp breads. Thane had also brought along two bottles of a rosé he knew she particularly liked. As she read the label her hand unconsciously stroked the windbreaker he had tossed casually across the console before he had gone back out.

She joined him on the bridge as they left the

sheltered marina. "Care to venture a guess as to where I'm taking you?"

"To meet Daddy's tanker?" She had put off calling her father, knowing how difficult it would be to talk knowing that anyone with the right radio frequency could listen in.

Thane's teasing smile warmed into something that quickened her pulses. "You lose. Pay the forfeit."

"You didn't mention any forfeit."

"You didn't ask," he parried.

The brilliant sunlight revealed a few silver threads among the darker gold at his temples, and Tally resisted the impulse to reach out and touch the crisp curls that broke free of his thick, silky thatch in that one particular area. "Six hundred and fifty-three dollars and seventy-nine cents, right?"

"Wrong. Just this once I'll let you off with a cup of coffee and a promise."

"Hmmm. You wouldn't settle for just coffee?" This time his eyes seemed bottomless, and she was in danger of drowning in the sparkling depths of them.

"Promise me that until we get home again, my pseudo-fiancée, you won't mention David or anything connected with the past." His strong brown hand made an infinitesimal movement on the throttle and twin screws bit into the water, throwing up a froth of blue-white suds behind them.

"Fair enough. We leave David to wrestle with the I-95 traffic. Now, what about *your* past, or is this a unilateral agreement?" she teased daringly. There was something invigorating about the clean salt air and it filled her veins with a subliminal excitement.

"My past, dear child, is a boring succession of schools and jobs and then more of the same. I'd be delighted to leave it behind."

She eyed him skeptically. "All right, but if you think I believe that, you're crazy. Don't forget, I've seen you in action." She could feel the flush start at her neck and work its way up to her hairline. "I mean with Judy," she blurted, turning to go below.

"I thought we were going to leave the past ashore."

"Whose side is she on, yours or mine? Or maybe she isn't the past, but the future," Tally snapped, reaching for the oiled teak door. It didn't help to see the sudden flash of amusement in Thane's eyes—amusement tinged with something thoughtful, something almost speculative. If he hadn't thought of Judy as the future before, then he obviously did now. Why in the devil couldn't she have kept her mouth shut?

By the time she had two mugs of coffee ready, her composure was intact. She was going to enjoy this outing if it killed her. Adjusting her smile to the proper degree of pleasant impersonal interest, she went topside and handed Thane his steaming mug. "Oh, there's the old Ripley place. I heard he used to keep a Chinese junk moored there."

From there the conversation moved to an exhibit of Chinese jades she and Maddie had seen at the Norton Gallery, which led to a discussion of the Taylors, themselves. While Tally studied the salt-hazed shape of Lake Worth Coast Guard Station on Peanut Island, Thane went on to discuss his plans for the rest of the week. "I'll want Cartwright to meet my operations chief at the Orlando plant—might need to check in at the main office, as well. It would have suited me better to have Tom take a more active role in setting up an Australian operation, but he flatly refused to be transplanted."

"Maddie doesn't want him taking on any more responsibility."

With one hand on the wheel, Thane allowed his glance to flicker over her. "They both liked you enormously, you know."

"Did they?" Her fingers traced the Imari design on the outsized cup. "I liked them enormously, too." She was glad he didn't bring up the other couple, for she simply hadn't been able to warm up to the Evynses. Not that it mattered. She'd never see either couple again.

"Better watch it. I don't want you parboiled again," Thane reminded her. She had rolled up her sleeves, and her forearms were beginning to show a pink tint already.

She rolled them down again and moved back to watch their course through Palm Beach Inlet. From her vantage point she had a perfect view of Thane's back, and she studied him as he handled the controls with practiced ease. Obviously not *all* his waking hours were spent in his office. That permanent bronze tan, for instance, didn't come from smoke-filled board rooms.

He spoke without turning around. "Aren't you curious about where we're going?"

She moved up beside him again and studied the compass as if the numbers opposite the lubber's line meant something to her. "Oh-nine-oh. Then we're headed for the Canary Islands," she intoned gravely.

"That's a possibility if we miss the set of the Gulf Stream and end up north of Manitilla Shoal," he grinned.

"Nova Scotia via the Bermuda triangle?" she ventured, inhaling the sun-warmed scent of his skin.

"I hope HouseSpouse never rents you out as a navigator." He swatted her on the bottom and she grabbed the offended area. "Go put some sunscreen on your nose, and while you're down there put the wine on ice if you didn't before. It ought to be just right by the time we drop anchor."

It was a day out of time, a sparkling jewel of a day that blew away the remnants of the past and the uncertainties of the future to leave only a present that glistened with expectancy. The sea was as calm as a teapot and there were a few puffy clouds overhead that looked like blobs of whipped topping in a cobalt bowl.

About two hours out, Thane cut both engines and allowed them to drift closer to a small sand island before dropping anchor in the transparent waters.

"Where on earth are we? Or rather, where at sea?" Tally asked wonderingly. She had been dozing under the sun shade for the past hour, and now she leaned over the side, seeing nothing more then a long, low-lying sandbar with a ruffle of scrubby vegetation along its spine.

"Shall we go ashore and plant a flag?" While she slept, Thane had stripped down to a pair of brief white trunks, and she had to force her gaze away from his magnificent body. It was unfair of the man to have everything! Looks, money, intelligence and that indefinable something that acted on a woman's internal magnet like a steel pylon.

"Go on, change into your bathing suit. You did bring one, didn't you?"

She scrambled below, suddenly impatient to dive into those clear, inviting waters. Never a real exercise freak, she felt an uncharacteristic urge to swim until she was totally exhausted.

They waded ashore a few minutes later and Tally laughed as she hopped about on the blistering sand. Thane grabbed her arm and tugged her back to the edge of the water, where they sat in the shallows, allowing the cooling wavelets to lap over their legs. "We'll have to picnic on board," he told her, reaching out to lift her wet hair and frown at her pale shouders. "One of these days, you're going to have to take the time to get a decent base coat so you won't blister after five minutes' exposure."

Ignoring him, she asked, "Where are we, anyway?" She forced her gaze away from the drops of moisture that glistened on his surprisingly dark chest hair and studied her small white toes through the distorting lens of the water.

"Probably twelve or fifteen miles north of Freeport. Shall we christen this island Tally Shoals?"

She flopped over on her stomach and stared at him again. "Freeport! Thane, what are we doing out here?" She had never been to the Bahamas. It seemed ridiculous that they could take a casual spin and wind up so near the British-owned islands.

With no warning, he rolled over to lie beside her in the shallow water. One arm reached out and he turned her to face him. "Can't you think of any good reason why I might want to get you off on a deserted island to myself?"

"None unless you mean to maroon me out here and ask for a refund from HouseSpouse. I think I've been more of a liability than an asset," she said ruefully, ignoring the turbulence inside her. She couldn't look away from his eyes, and she couldn't look into them, and the confusion was tearing her apart!

"I thought we'd declared a moratorium on all old business," he murmured. Propped up on one elbow, as she was, he was holding her loosely, his gaze ranging over her face, her shoulders, her breasts in the thin nylon jersey suit. She shivered in spite of the ninety-degree temperatures and the blistering sun that beat down on them even through the water.

"You're not cold?" he murmured.

"A goose walked over my grave." But it had nothing to do with superstition, it was plain old chemistry—the same chemistry he had warned her about. The warning hadn't been strong enough.

A roughness edged his voice as he told her it was time to go back aboard for lunch. Not waiting for her, he rose to his feet with an agility that was beautiful to watch, and dived out to where the bottom dipped abruptly. By the time Tally reached for the boarding ladder, he was already aboard, and he caught at her wrist with more strength than necessary and hauled her up.

One glance at his closed face and she turned away. All right, if he wants to revert to type, then that's fine with me, Tally told herself as she rubbed her hair vigorously before slipping on her denim shirt. There was no audience out here. They could forget the need to keep up that silly pretense.

Thane had lunch already spread out on the chart table when she went below. Neither of them had spoken since coming back to the *Pearl Fisher*, and she took her place silently, conquering an urge to turn around and go back outside.

He filled the wineglasses and she stared at the tea-rose pink liquid as it sloshed ever so gently with the motion of the boat. "I thought we'd better get in out of the sun during the hottest part of the day," he explained tersely, as if reluctant to break the silence.

She merely nodded, allowing him to serve her with the lobster salad.

"Crackers? Anchovy spread?"

Her voice still worked. Somehow, she was surprised. "No thank you, not now." This was absurd! But once embarked on a course, she found it almost impossible to veer. For her troubles, she had to suffer Thane's mocking gaze on her the whole time she choked down the food on her plate.

When she unobtrusively blotted the persiration from her neck with her shirt collar, Thane stood up and flicked a few switches. Somewhere an engine hummed into life, and soon she felt a welcome stream of cool air playing over her. "Thank you," she managed stiffly.

"Don't mention it." His eyes mocked her openly now, and she cringed at the contradicting emotions that flooded through her. He had had three glasses of wine to her one, and when he pushed his plate aside, she rose wordlessly and began repacking the hamper and stacking the dishes in the tiny stainless steel sink. Her hands welcomed the task; her mind was not so fortunately engaged.

From the corner of her eye she saw him lean out and put his unlit cheroot in a gimbaled ashtray, and then he turned to her, eyes narrowed and mouth grimly set. He reached for her and there was nowhere to retreat.

"Thane, stop it—this is absurd!" Her backward step brought her up against the padded locker that served as a couch during the day, a berth at night, and he followed her down as she lost her balance. "The dishes—" she yelped, reaching wildly for any excuse she could find to prevent from happening just what she wanted so desperately.

He made a rude suggestion as to the disposal of the dishes.

Her halfhearted protest was shut off as his mouth

came down on hers, and then it flew out of her mind as her senses wrested control from her intellect. He acted like a man who had reached the limits of endurance. His kiss seemed more an expression of anger, of frustration, than of desire, but then there was a subtle change. Somewhere along the line, force gave way to seduction, and as his hands began to play a beguiling game of their own, she moaned against the moist sweetness of his mouth and the last of her resistance melted away.

Her very bones melted. Molten lava coursed along her veins as she felt the straps of her bathing suit pushed down over her arms. What had happened to her shirt? What had happened to his? What had happened to the common sense that had guided her life for so long?"

"Thane, this is impossible," she implored, her fingers twisting in his hair as he slowly turned her nipples into small peaks of ecstasy with his lips, his teeth and his tongue.

"Nothing is impossible today," he avowed hoarsely, directing his attention farther south. "Nothing and no one exists except the two of us, here and now."

"Ah-h-h, Thane, please." The sound was barely audible, her ambiguous words no match for the tremors that shook her when he tugged her suit over her hips and lifted her enough to draw it off.

"Oh, my lovely, lovely precious," he groaned. He took her eager hands then and guided them slowly down his flanks. As her fingers curled into his hard, resiliant flesh, he groaned and turned away, his eyes closed tightly and his breath tearing from tortured lungs. Her eyes clung helplessly to his strong profile, wordlessly pleading, and then with a sharp sigh he came to her again. Tasting, tantalizing, teasing, he buried his face in the quivering softness of her cool, pale body.

She waited for the heavens to be split asunder and take her inside, but when the split came, it was from another kind of heaven.

Her fingers had just discovered the tiny nailheads of his masculine nipples and she heard his indrawn gasp just as thunder rocked the boat. At first she connected it with Thane, with the harsh sound of his breathing. Then she heard the second deep-throated rumble following almost immediately, felt him stiffen against her, and then the cabin was lighted with a brilliant blue-white flash.

"We must have made a few of the ancient gods jealous," Thane grated, rolling to his feet in one lithe movement. Without so much as a backward glance, he was through the hatch, leaving her staring after him, aching and devastated.

They skirted to the southwest of the squall line, making good time in spite of the growing choppiness. Tally, after dragging on her jeans and shirt, had taken one look at her shattered face in the small mirror and turned away with a soft oath. It was all there to see. He'd take one look at her and know! If she could have stayed below for the next three years, she would have considered it, but the way they were rolling, she knew she'd only be piling on the misery. Seasickness would be the last straw!

But she hated the vulnerability she saw mirrored in her eyes—hated even more what she had learned about herself today.

Thane called down to her. "Better make some coffee. We'll need it to clear away the effects of the wine!" *The wine!* The twin engines surged eagerly ahead under his skilled hand, and Tally turned leadenly to the minute galley.

Torrential rains met them halfway and followed them on in. At least Thane had his hands too full to do more than send her a quick, concerned glance as she brought him a mug of steaming coffee. "Better get below. You'll be drenched."

"I don't mind," she countered dully. "It's better than being seasick."

He nodded, his attention already claimed in searching out the channel markers as they approached the inlet again.

The next day Tally took the women on a round of the shops. They sighed and coveted their way along Worth Avenue, and then she took them to several of the best of West Palm's department stores, pointing out places of interest along the way. By the time they staggered in under the piles of boxes and parcels, it was time to dash off to the kitchen to check with Waldo and Mrs. Hume.

She had managed to avoid all but the briefest contact with Thane, but she had been aware on more then one occasion of his enigmatic eyes following her around. It was harder to stay busy now that Mrs. Hume was back in action, but she did her best. She'd wind up these last few days in fine style if it killed her, and then she'd catch a bus and go back to Otter Creek. There was probably no one there she even knew anymore, but it was a starting place.

Judy came back late Friday night. They had just finished dinner when she strolled into the East Room and flopped on one of the sofas, as much at home in Thane's house as if she had lived there all her life. "Don't ever let anyone tell you modeling isn't drudgery. I'm bushed! Thane, love, would you fix me a gin and tonic? I can't move another inch!"

It was after Thane had handed her the tall frosty

glass that he turned to Tally. "Did I tell you that we'll be taking off early in the morning? After an hour or so in Orlando, we'll head on up to New York and probably stay overnight. I'll let you know when I see how our schedule goes, all right?"

It was to Tally that he directed the words, but it was Judy who leaned forward eagerly, all signs of exhaustion magically erased. "Thane, dear brother-in-law-to-be, would this by any chance be a company plane?"

He lifted a dark, quizzical eyebrow in her direction. "It would."

"Darling, would you have room for one more passenger? I've simply *got* to get to New York, and I was dreading the hassle of a commercial flight. I always end up squeezed onto that shuttle out of National, and I swore the last time . . ." Her voice trailed off beguilingly and she widened her eyes at him. Tally could have throttled her!

There was room, of course. There was even room in the Jag that Thane planned to drive to Orlando, where he'd pick up the company jet. Had there not been, he would have taken the Bentley, Tally was sure—if Hume would have allowed him to drive it.

It was Judy who entertained them all at an early breakfast the following morning with a list of her favorite haunts in New York, and it was Judy who ran her hands caressingly up Thane's chest to straighten his tie when they gathered outside a short while later to see the three men and Judy on their way north. Thane was dressed in an impeccably cut pale gray suit, with a tie one shade darker. He looked almost as formidable as he had that first night Tally had laid eyes on him, and she stood off to one side, feeling tongue-tied, miserable and bereft. Pam and Debbie waved and went back inside, and Judy slid into the front seat beside the driver's place, but Thane hesitated, studying Tally with a coolly questioning look. He strolled the few feet to where she lingered, a parody of a smile hanging onto her face by a thread.

"You've been awfully quiet, sweetheart," he murmured, so softly that Tally didn't see why he even bothered. He had his back to the others; surely there was no more need for pretense. "Can you hold the fort for a couple more days? I wouldn't be taking off this way unless it was absolutely necessary."

"Of course I can," she retorted, not quite meeting his eyes. "After all, that's what I was hired for, isn't it?"

Thane studied her dispassionately for a moment. "Come on, darling—give your lover a proper send-off."

"Consider yourself sent."

He took her hands, turning them over to trace the blue veins on the inner sides of her wrists. "Put them around my neck where they belong."

"Take a hike," she muttered rudely, and his fingers tightened on her wrists.

"You're fond of giving me my marching orders, aren't you? No wonder Loggins traded you in on a more amenable model. For a loving fiancée, you leave a lot to be desired."

"May I return the compliment?" she retorted sweetly.

She had forgotten the nearby audience. Evidently, Thane had not. He caught her to him and ground a punishing kiss into her lips, taking great pleasure, she had no doubt, in hurting her. Lifting his head a moment later, he said loudly, "That will have to last me until tomorrow, beloved. I'll call you tonight."

That'll have to last you until hell freezes over,

Tally thought wretchedly as she watched the low-slung car disappear between the giant century plants that guarded the gate. She swallowed painfully and turned her blurred gaze toward the house. There was breakfast to clear away, her room to do, and the entertainment to arrange for the two women left behind.

All right, Tally Fitzsimmons, you've prided yourself on your level-headedness; let's see you put your act together and get it on the road.

She went through the motions, but it was as if the mainspring was missing. More sight-seeing, more shopping, arranging to have most of the purchases shipped home. She picked up a special order for Waldo and the mended tureen from the repair shop. She did fresh flowers for every room in the house and then went through the linens for the housekeeper, to track down a missing cutwork tablecloth.

Anything and everything to keep her thoughts from dwelling on Thane and Judy. Thane called and, as it happened, Lucy answered the phone. She gestured to Tally, but Tally shook her head. "Can't talk now—take the message!" She dashed off toward the back of the house as if she were on some desperate lifesaving mission.

As perhaps she was.

Chapter Nine

When she heard the low growl of the Jaguar the following morning just before noon, Tally was in the foyer sweeping up the fallen petals from under an arrangement of stephanotis and anthurium. She moved to the doorway, a reluctant welcoming committee of one, while Judy supervised the collection of several packages and Thane and Ed retrieved the bags from the trunk. Seeing Tally waiting, David strolled up the two wide steps, his jacket slung over his shoulder. Oddly enough, it was the nearest they had come to being alone since his arrival. His smile was tentative, but when hers rose spontaneously to her lips, his eyes warmed in relief.

"Hi, Savalas." David greeted her automatically with the familiar old play on her name.

Tally's response was just as automatic. She reached up and tugged the loosened knot of his tie. "Hi, Giant Slayer—how's the slingshot concession?"

It was as if a wordless apology had been asked, a wordless absolution given. And then Tally's smile withered and died as it met with an icy blast from Thane's narrowed eyes.

Pam and Debbie emerged from the guest quarters to greet their men, and suddenly Thane was looming over Tally's shoulder like a seething thunderhead.

"Hello, darling. Too busy to give your fiancé a welcome home kiss?" His voice was heavy with the old mockery.

Tally shot him a sidelong glare and turned to stalk off, but his hand caught her elbow before she had gone three feet.

The angry protest hung in her throat as Judy sauntered over to drape an arm across both their shoulders. Heaving a theatrical sigh, she said, "D'you suppose we could drop the Astrodome over the whole island and air-condition it? Even the few feet between the car and the house are too much! I'm wilted! How about you, darling? After last night I'm amazed you can even hold your eyes open!" She turned to Tally. "By the way, George and Jessica sent their regards. We were with them until all hours, weren't we, Thane? Did you know, Tally, that Jessica has a teeny-weeny crush on our Thane?" Her voice grew insufferably kittenish. "It's a good thing he had me along the whole time to keep him pure."

The look Thane sent Judy wasn't much better than the one he had favored Tally with, but it served to dilute his attention for a second. Tally almost managed to escape, but once more he caught her before she had gone more than a few steps, and this time he yanked her into the study, slamming the door behind them.

"All right now, suppose you tell me what's wrong!" he demanded grimly.

"Nothing's wrong—at least, not with me, it isn't! Just because I don't come running to fawn all over you, your rotten temper breaks out like a bad case of hives!"

"Speaking of rotten tempers, your own is nothing to brag about," Thane retorted. "And while we're on the subject of fawning, how about restraining yourself from climbing all over Loggins—at least while his wife is standing there looking as if a mule had just kicked her!"

"I didn't, and she wasn't! I only straightened his tie—the way Judy straightened yours before you left—and furthermore, it's none of your business if I want to . . . to seduce him on the courthouse square!"

"You try any more cute little games and I'll show you whose business it is," Thane said in a dangerously soft tone. "We've got one more day to get through and, so help me, if I catch you with Loggins one more time, you'll be sorry."

"Catch me!" Tally exploded. "*Catch* me! Oh . . . Oh! You have a terrific opinion of me, don't you? I should have known you hadn't changed one bit from that f-first night when you accused me of—of—" Flags of temper were flying high in her cheeks as her blazing eyes bored into Thane's narrowed ones. "You're in no position to be threatening me, Thane Coulter. I've kept my part of the bargain to the letter, and I'm just counting the minutes until tomorrow so I can get away from this place!"

"And go where?" he demanded witheringly.

Her chin lifted. "Don't worry about it—you won't be stuck with me. I have a place to go."

"Have you forgotten we're meeting your father in Tampa next week?"

For a wonder, she had. She had forgotten everything except the instinctive need to get as far away as possible from a situation that threatened to maim her for life. "I—I'll meet him alone. There's no reason for you to concern yourself with my affairs any longer. Our contract ends tomorrow."

His fingers flexed as if he could hardly prevent himself from digging them into her. Taking a deep breath, he reminded her. "He thinks we're engaged."

"So? Believe me, if any man knows about broken relationships, Rex does! Look, Thane, I know you mean well," she said earnestly, ignoring his angry, baffled expression, "but your deal with Cartwright is more or less sewed up by now, isn't it? There's just no point in dragging this farce out any longer." She struggled to tug the sapphire and diamond ring from her finger and then Thane caught her hands and crushed the bones in his iron grip.

"This farce, as you call it, managed to save your stiff-necked pride, in case you've forgotten," he reminded her forcefully. "Forgive me if I misunderstood the situation, but it appeared to me that you were so idiotically in love with that half-baked puppy you'd appreciate having a man to hide behind when he dumped you to marry the boss's daughter!"

They glared at each other relentlessly. The grayness underlying Thane's deep tan nagged Tally's conscience, but his eyes, black with anger, triggered her stubbornness. She ought to simply walk off the job! Meeting his glare head on, she refused to give him the satisfaction, and evidently something of her turbulent feelings reached him. Some of the tension seemed to drain from him. He flexed his shoulders and eyed her bleakly. "Did you think all this was purely for Cartwright's sake?" His voice was edged with sarcasm. "Good Lord, grant me the ability to conduct my business affairs without the help of some wide-eyed female with a good line in sob stories! If I'd had any sense, I'd have put you clean out of my mind after that first preposterous business with Hiram!"

There was a pulse pounding heavily at his temple and Tally stared at it hypnotically, her eyes like bruises in her white face. "So why didn't you?"

The pulse slowed even as she watched, and her gaze moved unwillingly to his eyes and hung there until the familiar shutters came down. Thane shook his head slowly, turning away. "Lord only knows."

Free from the compelling gaze, she could only stand there, staring at his stern profile and *aching*. As if he felt her eyes on him, he shot her a look, and she met it unflinchingly. Then, defeated, she sagged and turned away.

"Tally?" The tone was no longer angry. If she hadn't known better, she might have thought it was . . . hesitant. Almost apologetic.

"What?" she asked dully without turning around.

His hands came down on her shoulders again, gently for once, and he pulled her back against his solid strength. There was no more enmity. It was as if the furious exchange of words had drained them both. Not that they had solved anything; not that they ever could.

All the same, when Thane turned her to face him she didn't resist, although her only expression was a sort of weary resignation. And then, as if he couldn't help himself—as if the laws of gravity were too powerful to resist—he lowered his mouth to hers, and she rationalized shamefully, telling herself that this was one way to prove her utter indifference to him.

It was a strange kiss, almost totally devoid of passion. When Thane moved with her to sink into a deep leather chair, she remained passive, both her hands lying loosely in her lap, her head unresistingly on his shoulder. His mouth touched hers again, brushing lightly, tentatively over the surface without attempting to break through her apathy.

But then gradually, imperceptibly, the tenor changed. His body stirred beneath her and his hand on her thigh tightened. He began to stroke her hip, and his tongue flicked out to caress her lips, and she stiffened.

As if in response to her withdrawal, he drew back immediately. "God, I'm too exhausted for this sort of thing," he muttered, his voice rough and slightly unsteady. "What I need is a bath, a double whiskey and about twelve hours of sleep."

Rousing from her strange inertia, Tally was once more stung into action. She pushed herself off his lap. "Then please—don't let me waste any more of your valuable time!"

She was already at the door when his heavy response caught her. "Can we table this argument until later, Tally? I'm not sure which one of us was winning when the troops gave out—at least, this troop did—but I promise you, we'll pick up where we left off as soon as the battlefield is cleared of unauthorized personnel."

Tally was already castigating herself for a weak, greedy fool. As if she had been in a trance of some sort, she had sat there and let him make love to her again! Talk about a hair of the dog!

She made it to her bedroom without meeting any

of the others, luckily. Her shirttail was out, her hair was a mess, and her eyes—! Staring at her haunted image in the bathroom mirror, she wondered if this was what a victim of shell shock looked like. Surely the feeling must be similar.

She splashed her face and wrists in cold water—as if it could help. It wasn't her temper this time. Her anger had been swallowed up by a much more compelling emotion, and it was going to take a lot more than cold water to relieve this particular malady.

She was brushing her disheveled hair back behind her ears when she heard sounds of someone in the room beyond. Her hand stilled. Surely he wouldn't barge in on her now to continue where they had left off. Wherever that had been. Fighting? Making love? Where did one end and the other begin?

On the other hand, it wouldn't hurt to flip the latch on the connecting door. Her hand was reaching for the knob when the door opened and Judy came in, trailing a pair of panty hose and a striped silk scarf from her fingers.

"Hi, doll. Did you and Thane bury the hatchet?"

Tally shot her a baleful glare. The last thing she needed now was a little sisterly commiseration. "What were you doing in Thane's room?"

"Just checking to be sure I hadn't left any of my things in his overnight bag." She dangled the hose and scarf playfully. "Can you see old lady Hume's face if she pulled out a pair of hose from between Thane's shirts and socks? She'd turn purple!"

"Judy, I don't want to hear about it," Tally said flatly.

"Don't want to hear about what, love? Thane's and my night . . . on the town?"

"Look, it's time for lunch and the Cartwrights will

be wondering where everyone is. Would you mind checking with Mrs. Hume? I'll be out in a minute." The thought of food was enough to make her ill, but the thought of Thane and Judy sharing a . . . a night of any sort was infinitely worse!

Judy's blue-gray eyes narrowed speculatively. She had evidently removed her contacts as soon as she had arrived. "What's the matter, did you get your walking papers? I could have told you, sweets, that no employer will put up with insolence. How long were you contracted for, anyway?"

"Judy, just get out of my room, will you?" Tally seethed. She was going to bawl any minute now, and she didn't want any witnesses.

The tall blonde sauntered across to the door that opened out onto the terrace. "Your room, Tally?" she called provocatively over her shoulder. "I wouldn't push my luck, doll. Just because Thane hired you to dress up and play lady for his friends doesn't mean anything. And Tally, in case he wandered into the wrong bed a few times, don't try to turn it into something it's not. Believe me, I know this particular breed of man. The high pressure they live under has to find an outlet now and then, and you were handy."

"Will you please just go?" Tally managed through stiff lips. If there was more, she didn't want to hear it. Judy had told her nothing she didn't already know.

Waldo, his red face beaming under his paper hat, offered her a triumphant grin as he stirred the bouillabaisse. He had outdone himself for the Cartwright's last dinner. MacGregor had offered her his choicest blossoms, too—for some obscure reason, the cantankerous Scot had taken to her. Even Faye and Lucy were on their best behavior. It was a shame that Mrs. Hume's back seemed to be acting up again, but Tally had made up her mind that nothing was going to prolong her stay one minute longer than necessary. She'd see the guests on their way, surpervise putting the guest rooms back in order, and that was it.

Hanging the smock she wore in the kitchen on its hanger, she hurried to her room to change for dinner. To her dismay, Judy was already there, trying on the sapphire earrings. Mocking turquoise eyes met angry blue ones in the mirror, and Judy said, "Pity these don't match. Maybe something in the line of aquamarines would be better. They aren't as valuable, but even so, good ones—"

"Judy, take them off. What are you doing in here, anyway?"

"The light's not good in the apartment. I need a better mirror for my makeup, so don't be selfish."

Tally yanked the fern print chiffon from the closet and drew it on over her head. She had showered earlier, and already she felt in need of another, but there wasn't time. The trick was to keep from getting so steamed up.

The trick was to put Thane Coulter and Judy and the whole east coast of Florida behind her, as far and as fast as she could! Defiantly she scrabbled through her top drawer and came up with the small dime store pearl earrings she had brought with her. If Thane had any objections, he could darned well choke on them.

Not that he'd even see her with Judy in the same room, she thought dismally. She had seldom been jealous of anyone, but for once she wished she were taller. Five-feet-five was such an insignificant height to be—neither tall enough to be striking, nor short enough to be called petite. And there was the matter of her coloring—no matter how carefully she applied her makeup, it didn't suit her. In this mood, nothing would! Frowning down at the delicate fern print chiffon, she felt like a shadow beside her tall, vibrant stepsister.

Beside her Judy pressed her lips together to spread her frosted lipstick. Smiling slyly at Tally's reflection, she said, "What do you bet that I end up with the ring, the earrings and the whole shooting match within a week after you leave?"

"Aren't you leaving tomorrow, too?" Tally was startled into asking.

One tanned shoulder moved sinuously under the peacock silk straps. "Why should I leave just when things are beginning to get interesting? Unlike you, sister dear, I'm a guest. It would be a shame if everybody walked out at once and left poor Thane here all by his lonesome, wouldn't it?"

Determinedly, Tally forced herself to ignore the taunts. She had been subjected to Judy's particular brand of provocation since high school days. It had been hard, but she had learned to put it into perspective and go on about her business. And business, she reminded herself, was the only thing that was keeping her here.

Moving with a swift grace, she closed the bedroom door quietly behind her and paused, eyes closed momentarily, to take a steadying breath. *Hang in there, darn it—it won't be long now.*

She opened her eyes to see Thane emerging from his own door farther along the hall, and for a moment she panicked. She was halfway down the hall when he caught up with her. "Tally, wait!"

She didn't even bother to glance at him. Her eyes focused resolutely on the design in the silky Tabriz runner, she marched ahead.

He swore and caught at her arm. "Tally, slow down, will you?"

Looking pointedly at her arm, where his dark fingers contrasted so markedly with her own much paler flesh, she steeled herself to confront him, chin lifted belligerently and eyes as hard as star sapphires. "Make it quick. Mrs. Hume isn't feeling well and I need to see to dinner."

"I hire a staff to see to dinner!" he thundered impatiently, and she shot him a coolly triumphant look.

"Exactly."

"Look, Tally—" He released her when she lowered a meaningful glance at the square-tipped fingers that bit into her arm. And then, idiot that she was, it was all she could do not to reach for his hand and place it on her arm again. "Tally, I seem to be forever apologizing to you. Believe me, I'm usually the most even-tempered, level-headed fellow around, but for some reason . . ." He shook his head. His smile was disarming, and Tally steeled herself against being disarmed. She was already badly outgunned in this obscure battle they seemed to be waging.

"Really, Mr. Coulter, I understand perfectly. I'm sure the pressures of business—"

The stream of profanity that followed broke off with a plea for forbearance. "Tally, look, you've misunderstood the whole thing from the beginning. If it's any comfort to you, I've been just about as bad, but after tonight—"

"Mr. Coul—" As the thick dark eyebrows closed over the bridge of his proud nose to form a solid, threatening bar, Tally swallowed and reconsidered. "Thane, I'm sure the matter of a . . . a few kisses means no more to you than it did to me. This sort of thing just . . . happens. It happens all the time. Goodness knows, I certainly don't attach any importance to something so trivial." Her tone was so brittle she was surprised her tongue wasn't bleeding. She topped it off with a blinding smile and turned away, willing her feet to proceed at a decorous rate of speed until she rounded the corner and could no longer feel his eyes flaying the flesh from her very bones.

Moments later she was in the dining room making a last-minute check of the table setting when she heard the door to the study slam. For an instant she froze, a footed rock crystal goblet in her hand. So Thane's ego was having problems with words like "trivial" and "unimportant." The thought brought a tiny smile to her lips, and then common sense returned. She checked the goblet against the light and replaced it with one that wasn't water spotted. If Thane was sulking in the library, she felt compelled to go find the guests and see if they wanted something to drink before dinner. Waldo had given her a twelve-minute deadline and she had learned not to try and stretch it.

"Hi. Where is everyone?" Her eyes swept the room and found only David, relaxing on the sofa.

He remained seated. "Oh, hi, Savalas. Deb's doing something to her hair and the C's are packing. I don't know where the head honcho is—counting his gold, probably." His laugh was a little brash and Tally marveled at how young and unsure of himself David seemed now. When he had left her to fly out to Australia he had been a giant of a man whose stride had covered two continents.

"David," she said earnestly, "I'd like to give you back your ring and your picture." She sat gingerly on the end of the sofa and turned to face him. This would be her last chance to tidy up the loose ends of their old relationship. She had to do something with both items, and she couldn't see lugging them around for the rest of her days.

"Ah, Tal, that's not necessary, honest," he protested halfheartedly.

"But I want to! Really, David, it's a lovely ring, and who knows, some day your own son might need it." She grinned impishly as an irreverent thought occurred to her. "The picture will make a perfect gift for Debbie—it's already inscribed with the proper sentiments."

David bunched a playful fist under her chin and she giggled; and then Thane was there, casting a blight over the whole room. Tally stood up, her social mask in place, and walked sedately past him to greet Pam and Ed Cartwright. "There's just time for a swallow of sherry before Waldo serves notice on us."

Only by reminding herself frequently that tonight was the last of these occasions was Tally able to get through the meal. The dinner itself was a splendid tribute to Waldo's self-professed genius, and the service, for once, was flawless. She rather thought both Faye and Lucy had ideas of applying to House-Spouse for positions as soon as they could escape from the Humes' watchful eye.

But from the head of the table, Thane seemed to follow her every move. If she reached for her wineglass, his eyes bored into her so that she put it down untasted. If she touched a fork to the delectable thyme-seasoned veal, she lost her nerve before she could lift it to her tongue.

Or was it only her hypersensitive imagination? How could any man sit there and carry on an intelligent conversation with his guests and at the same time manage to reduce her to a state of near catalepsy? She was just being self-conscious, imagining his eyes following her every move, her every nuance of expression.

They were comparing notes on their respective boats, and she tuned in to the conversation in time to hear Ed's genial invitation to visit them in Queensland. "We've got a place at Surfer's Paradise. Can't compare with this little heap of yours, Thane, but we like it, all the same. Fishing's tops—surfing if you care for that sort of thing. Me, I'll settle for a rod, a chair, and a couple of cold ones, anyday."

Under the swell of conversation, David leaned over and whispered that he may as well take the picture and the ring if she was sure she didn't mind.

"Sure I'm sure," Tally answered softly, with a smile that was warmer than she knew, purely as a reaction to the tension she was under.

Her answer was smothered under a burst of general laughter, and David leaned closer again. "What did you say?"

Shaking her head helplessly, Tally mouthed the word "later." She turned to listen with feigned fascination at the Cartwrights went over their hastily revised plans for the rest of their stay in the States. She ignored Thane's contemptuous glare. It was probably just a figment of her imagination, anyway. Men with eyebrows like his always looked slightly ferocious.

She forced herself to chime in when everyone

began listing points of interest along the eastern seaboard. The Australians had declared their intention of renting a car and driving all the way up the coast. "Can't waste a chance to compare your barrier reef to ours, you know, and the girls still have us in thumbscrews for leaving them behind the other day. Pam'la hasn't quite managed to bankrupt me yet, so I'll give her a whack at your Fifth Avenue, and then we'll head home to recover."

At an imperceptible nod from Thane, Tally rose and led the exodus to the East Room for coffee. She found herself walking alone as the three couples fell in behind her, and her head lifted instinctively to add another inch to her ramrod back. Her frozen expression warmed into a genuine smile as Hume entered through another door bearing the great Georgian silver coffee service. He wouldn't trust it to either Faye or Lucy, and Mrs. Hume wasn't lifting things these days.

"Thank you, Hume. I appreciate it." The versatile chauffeur promised to clear it away before he turned in, and Tally nodded and began to pour as the others settled themselves around the room with the ease of long familiarity. She had to admit that Thane was an excellent host—as well as a shrewd businessman. The Cartwrights could have been installed in any one of Palm Beach's incomparable hotels and entertained royally, all without once setting foot in the Coulter household. Instead, he chose to treat them almost as family.

Better than family, she thought wryly, remembering poor Hiram and Francis. She made a mental note to call them before she left West Palm for good.

Still, it would all pay off in the end. Disarmed by all the personalized hospitality, Ed would be a much easier proposition when the two of them met again in a conference room somewhere, both armed with a battery of lawyers.

By then, she'd be long gone. The business page of the *Times* might carry a notice of a deal between Coulter International and a certain Queensland oil concern, but by then she'd be able to read the name without feeling that heart-deep, unassuageable ache. If she could escape with her pride intact, that, at least, was something.

Sipping the reviving liquid, Tally allowed her eyes to range lovingly over the room she had grown so fond of in an incredibly short time. She'd miss it. Of all the homes she had worked in, this was the only one she had felt such an immediate affinity for. Catching Debbie's eyes, she smiled warmly, and then her gaze moved on to David and she hurriedly looked away. But she deliberately kept her eyes from straying to where Thane carried on a low-voiced conversation with Ed Cartwright.

One by one, the others wandered away. Pam and Debbie reluctantly returned to the impossible task of cramming all their last-minute purchases into the available luggage, and Judy mentioned something about checking to see if Claire had returned from Vegas. The men were talking business, and Tally took the opportunity to slip out and begin her own packing. Tomorrow was racing headlong toward her, and she needed to be able to get away with no messy delays.

The tiny engagement ring David had given her was wrapped in a handkerchief in the same drawer where she had placed his photograph. She removed them both and sat on the edge of the bed, smiling almost maternally at the gravely handsome face in the silver frame. "All my love forever, David," was scrawled across one corner. Ironic in light of subsequent events, but at least she could smile about it now without the slightest twinge.

A sound from the terrace made her glance up just as David walked in. "Hi. I thought you'd be coming back here pretty soon." He dropped down beside her on the bed with no more self-consciousness than if he were one of her high school girl friends. "That's it, huh?" Peering over her shoulder, he grinned wryly at his own image. "Saying good-bye to the old days?"

"I was going to wrap this and the ring and slip it to you in the morning before you all left."

"What, and have your beetle-browed boyfriend on my back? He watches you like a hawk, Tal. What do you see in him . . . besides the obvious, that is?" David picked the small diamond up and tossed it several times before putting it into his pocket.

"Depends on what you call the obvious." She'd just as soon skip a rehash of old times. It could only be embarrassing for both of them if David started asking for the particulars of her engagement.

"I guess all that lovely money can hide a few personality defects, but to tell you the truth, Tal, I was pretty shocked by the whole thing. I mean, after all, we . . ." His grimace brought a smile to her face. Poor David. He was a classic case of fox and sour grapes. Were all men so egotistical that they couldn't bear to have a woman turn them down first?

"Never mind, David, it all worked out for the best. Your Debbie's a darling. I hope you appreciate her, because she thinks the sun rises out of your eyes." There. Maybe if he knew which side his ego was buttered on, he'd hang on to what he had.

"Yeah, she's pretty neat, but Tally, I'll never forget you. I really loved you, you know, only . . . well, we were so far apart, and then Ed was so decent to me, and there was Debbie . . . It all just sort of happened." He shrugged.

She laid a hand over his. "I know, David. Please, don't worry about it. It was the same for me. I mean, you were there and Thane was here, and . . . So you see, neither of us has anything to regret."

His smile accepted her absolution and brightened perceptibly. "Well—guess I'd better get out of here before the house detective barges in on us."

Tally was only too willing. It occurred to her that Thane could as easily stroll in on them as David had, and she could trust him to misunderstand the whole innocent business. He had a talent for it.

"One for the road, Savalas," David teased, standing and pulling her to her feet. "For old times' sake."

Before she could protest he took her face in his hands and kissed her on the mouth, and it was as if she had kissed—Hiram. Or the gatepost. At least if there had been any lingering doubt, it was thoroughly exorcized.

Chapter Ten

So much for her early getaway! It was nine by the time the Cartwright's rental car was delivered. It was nine-thirty by the time it was discovered that no amount of manipulation was going to fit all that excess baggage into so small a space.

"As I see it, you have two choices," Thane observed. They were gathered in front of the house, all except Judy, who didn't rise before eleven. "You can either send around for a larger model, or you can repack and let us ship the excess on home for you. Tally will be glad to get it ready and Hume can take it into town tomorrow." He didn't look at her as he spoke, but Tally's sensitive ears didn't miss the slight hardening of his voice when he spoke her name. She must have seriously deflated his precious masculine ego.

In the face of Pam's prayerful relief, there was little Tally could do but acquiesce. Hume carried the various bags and parcels back inside, and the two Australian women spent three-quarters of an hour rearranging according to priority. It was almost eleven by then, and Judy wandered out to where the second attempt was being made to fit everything into the car.

"Still here? I thought you'd be halfway to Georgia by now."

The car finally crammed full, good-byes were said all around, and then Thane ushered Tally and Judy back inside. Tally had her own bags already packed and waiting in her room. She had unconsciously chosen to wear the same yellow two-piecer she had worn that first day two weeks ago.

Two weeks! Impossible to think that she had met Thane less than a month ago. Her whole life had changed completely since then—the earth had flipped on its axis.

Inventing an errand, she muttered an excuse and hurried toward the kitchen. She might as well say her good-byes before she phoned for a taxi. Faye, cap crooked on her brown curls and a stolen flower tucked into her apron pocket, caught up with her before she reached the door. "Tally, if you've got a minute, could you run across and see Aunt Hilda? She's flat on her back and fussing up a storm."

Hiding her frustration, Tally strode across the lush green backyard to the spacious garage apartment. At this rate, she'd never get out of here! She'd probably get to the end of the driveway to discover that West Indies Drive was being resurfaced and she was trapped for the duration!

Hilda Hume, a frown on her normally placid face, was worried about getting the house set back in order. "I know you were wanting to get home this morning, Tally, but if you could just see that the counterpanes are sent to the cleaners before you go . . . And while you're at it, would you mind closing off the study and throwing open all the windows? That place reeks of cigar smoke. If that don't do it, I'll get Hume to take down the draperies first thing next week."

And then there was lunch. Waldo had prepared her favorite meal, and his flushed face sagged pathetically when she told him she hadn't planned on staying for lunch. And of course, she relented. By the time first Faye and then Lucy had come to ask her about HouseSpouse, Inc., she was ready to think there must be some sort of conspiracy!

On her way to her room after a largely silent lunch—Thane had had a call and had to go out, according to Hume, and Judy was obviously sulking—she was accosted by MacGregor, who, to her knowledge, never ventured into the house.

"Won't be needin' any more of my flowers anytime soon, will ye? The cuttin' garden's gotta have time to recover."

She assured him that they could manage without cut flowers for a while, and thanked him for providing so beautifully, and the wiry, taciturn man grumbled something under his breath to the effect that he could manage a few lilies for her room if she'd a liking for them.

It was the last straw! She barely made it to her room before the floodgates opened. Throwing herself across the bed with no thought for her once crisp cotton dress, she howled. Darn, darn, *darn,* why did it have to be this way? She was even in love with old MacGregor! She was in love with the weathered, good-natured Hume, with his bustling little wife, and those two scatterbrained girls.

Unbidden, the image of Thane took shape in her mind. The changeable gray eyes that could shadow over so quickly, the dramatic contrast of his tanned skin, the sun-washed hair and those oddly dark brows. As if he were standing before her, she could feel the piercing intensity of his gaze, sense the coil-spring tension of his lean, hard body.

How *could* she have been so unutterably foolish as to fall in love with a man like Thane Coulter? Where was the cool, level-headed pragmatist who had picked herself up after each disaster and calmly gone about her affairs with no outward sign of the bleeding inside? Did she unconsciously invite this sort of thing? Was she one of those accident-prone individuals who went through life attracting trouble?

Rolling over to stare blindly up at the ceiling, she sniffed loudly and groped in her bedside drawer for a tissue. Enough of this maudlin self-pity. It really wasn't at all her style—at least, she hoped it wasn't. Here it was the middle of the afternoon and she had planned to be halfway across the state by now.

A bee droned heavily outside in the lantana bush. Somewhere in the house, a phone rang and was quickly answered. This sort of weather always made her drowsy, but there was no time now for self-indulgence. Outside, a brassy sun slanted down through the brooding Norfolk Island pines; it was hot and still and the atmosphere was laden with humidity—and at the rate she was going, she'd wind up in Otter Creek in the middle of the night in a blasted thunderstorm!

Once she forced her mind out of the rut of self-pity and focused it on her immediate situation, all thoughts of the weather faded away. Otter Creek! What had she been thinking of? It must have been an instinctive attempt to go back to a time when her life had been simple and secure; there was certainly nothing for her now in Otter Creek.

But there was in Tampa. Or there would be by the middle of the week—providing she could get there.

Problem number one: money. She had the last check her father had sent—still not cashed, unfortunately—and her savings account was certainly healthy enough. She could afford to take her time in looking around for just the right job, and there must be something she could do in Tampa. While she hadn't that many skills, she was certainly experienced when it came to management. What housekeeper of any standing wasn't?

Meanwhile, she had a slight cash-flow problem. More had flowed out than had flowed in over the past two weeks, and the banks wouldn't open until nine tomorrow morning. Which left her in an awkward spot unless Judy would be willing to lend her enough to get her to Tampa.

She slid off the bed, automatically pausing to smooth the spread again. Unfortunately, her dress was not so easily smoothed. Brushing out the worst of the wrinkles, she applied herself to her face and hair, disguising the ruinous traces of the past half hour. Then she braced herself to go find Judy.

After searching the house, she located her by the pool. "I thought you'd be gone," Judy said, stroking oil on her long, shapely legs. "Weren't you supposed to leave after lunch?"

"I was supposed to leave first thing this morning," Tally said dryly, dropping onto the foot of a cushioned lounge. "What with one thing and another . . ." She shrugged, considering the best way to approach an embarrassing subject.

"Mother called. I left a note saying where I was staying, and she just got in."

Tally couldn't bring herself to evince much interest. She felt nothing at all for the woman whose home she had shared for the past several years—not even anger. Claire's duplicity seemed small in comparison to other things that had taken place since.

"Well?" Judy lifted the pads over her eyes and blinked up at her. "Don't you want to hear the latest?"

She really didn't, but short of involving herself in a distasteful explanation, she had little choice. "Make it short. I still want to get away this afternoon."

"So who's stopping you? I just thought you might want to know that Claire's filing for divorce. So I guess that means we're no longer sisters, huh?"

The news barely made a dent in Tally's consciousness. As far as she was concerned, both Claire and Judy had ceased to be a part of her life. This just made it official. She must have made some appropriate sound, for Judy, her eyes covered again with the witch hazel pads, and her lean, perfectly proportioned body glistening like molten gold, continued drowsily.

"What's the matter with you? Finding it hard to tear yourself away from all this? Or is it Thane you can't bear to leave? Honey, I told you not to get involved with him. Thane's so far out of your league, you two aren't even playing the same game."

"It's nothing like that," Tally muttered hastily. The last thing she wanted was a cross-examination by Judy—or anyone else. "I just needed to ask a favor."

"That's a switch. You didn't even do that when we

were sisters. You're not upset about Mother, are you? Really, Tal, there was nothing left between her and Rex."

"Oh, I know that. Look, Judy, I've been in touch with Daddy. He's off the tug and working on a tanker. I don't know if it's a permanent switch or not, but—"

Removing her bra top and rolling onto her stomach, Judy said, "Nothing ever is with Rex, is it? Did he say what he's been up to all this time?"

Tally stood up. This was getting her nowhere. "Judy, I don't want to discuss Rex with you. What I need is . . . well, you see, I'm meeting him in Tampa about the middle of the week, and I need some money to tide me over."

"What happened to all your hope chest savings, or am I being tactless? And won't Thane pay you the going rate before you leave? Or did you take it out in clothes and other goodies?"

"I've got plenty of money in the bank," Tally returned, ignoring the jibe about her salary and attendant benefits, "but I can't get to it until the morning, and I wanted to leave town today. And I'll have to have a place to stay in Tampa. It shouldn't take long to transfer my account. In fact, I think there's a branch there."

Judy seemed to consider the request for several moments, raising Tally's hopes. "Well, sweetie, as much as I'd like to speed you on your merry way, I'm practically flat, myself, until I see Mother. I shot my wad in Vegas, and until Syd comes through with something from that Bimini gig, I can't afford to let loose a penny. Sorry. Why don't you try Sara Drummond? She can advance you something until she gets paid for this job, can't she?"

Tally bit her lip in irritation. Of course she could

ask Sara . . . and of course Sara would come through. All the same, it took time, and time was precisely what she didn't want to waste. She had no idea where Thane had gone, much less how long he'd be away, but it would be so much simpler if she could just clear out and be done with it. Given the mood she was in, she couldn't be responsible for her unruly tongue. The man had an unfortunate effect on her at the best of times.

"Thanks, anyway. I'll see if Hume can drop me off at Sara's apartment. And in case I don't see you again"—which I won't, she added silently—"good luck with school and your modeling career."

Judy, her long hair falling over her face like a golden waterfall, smiled lazily up at her. "Aren't you going to wish me luck with Thane, darling? I've decided not to go back to school. This place suits me to a T, in case you hadn't noticed."

Hume, patently disapproving her decision to leave before Thane got home, reluctantly promised to bring the Bentley around and Tally went to call Sara. She let the phone ring eleven times, unwilling to admit that her last hope had just gone down the drain. While she waited, growing more and more despondent, someone in the house picked up the receiver and then put it down again on finding it in use.

Well, drat! She sat there in the tiny room she had called her office for the past two weeks and wondered what on earth she could do now. Go sleep at the bus station until the bank opened? If she'd had any sense she would have transferred her account to a bank with an automatic teller, but no, she had to put it somewhere where it drew a quarter of a percent more interest! And now look where her foolish greediness had gotten her!

"The car's up front, Miss Tally," Hume interrupted her disgruntled thoughts apologetically. "Shall I take your bags out?"

She stared at him indecisively for a moment, hardly even seeing the kindly, weather-beaten face. She had to go somewhere, and she couldn't go back to Claire's. There was no telling when Sara would be in if she was off for the weekend with her yacht-broker friend.

"If you would, Hume," she answered absently. He could at least get her away from here, even if he only dropped her on the other side of the bridge. She'd think of something!

Not until they were clear of the entrance gates, with their guardian century plants, did he ask her where she was going, and then she hesitated a moment too long.

"Miss Tally, if I might suggest something," the uniformed man said diffidently. She had climbed into the front seat beside him, needing to prolong the friendly contact as long as possible. "Lucy said she thought you might be leaving town, and I just wanted to say . . . well, it's none of my business, but Mr. Hiram thinks the world of you, and I know he'd like to see you before you go—sort of say good-bye and all that."

Hiram! Or course! That big, delightful old mausoleum—those two lovely old men—even Mrs. Stoner's vinegary face would be a welcome sight! "You're absolutely right, Hume. I'd love to stop by there for a few minutes!"

She'd love to spend the night there, and what's more, she wouldn't be at all reluctant to invite herself! That's the last place Thane would think of looking for her.

But just in case she was wrong, when Hume carried her two bags to the broad verandah and pushed the buzzer, she made an effort to cover her tracks. "You don't have to wait, Hume. I'm going to call a friend—the woman I work for, actually—and she'll pick me up here. I can't tell you how much I appreciate this . . . and everything." Her chin was feeling wobbly again. "Say good-bye to everyone for me, Hume, and . . . and take care of yourself!"

She flung her arms around the startled man's waist and squeezed and then turned to greet Hiram Coulter's disgruntled-looking housekeeper.

Francis had an exotic new succulent from Africa to show her, and Hiram had just had a letter from Addie that he wanted to share. Even Mrs. Stoner allowed as how she could dump another cup of water in the soup if Miss Tally saw fit to eat with them.

"Make it sherry instead of water, Mrs. Stoner, and of course she's staying. She's going to take the front room and have a nice long vacation, aren't you, gal?" Hiram turned to her, his rheumy old eyes glowing with excitement, and Tally felt as if she'd come home to the grandfather she'd never known.

"Until tomorrow, at least, if I may."

They had dined exceedingly well on the potent terrapin soup, and Hiram was teaching her the rudiments of mah jong when Thane walked in. For several moments Tally could only stare at him. She was reminded so forcefully of the first time she had ever seen him; then, as now, he was strikingly attractive in stark black and white. Tonight he wore the white linen jacket and black knit shirt with a pair of well-cut khakis, and the whole ensemble looked as if he might have slept in it. His hair, that thick, palely gleaming crop, was as untidy as if he'd been caught in a windstorm, and his eyebrows met across the top of his proud nose like a solid line of thunderclouds.

"Thanks, Hiram," he said tersely, and then, "Tally, get your things together—now."

Which was precisely the wrong approach to take, especially as her volatile emotions were teetering on a tightrope between despair and pure, idiotic joy. "Hello, Thane. Sorry I didn't get to say good-bye before I left, but you were out."

"Are you going to do as I say?" His tone had already lit the short fuse to her temper, but she hung on, forcing herself to smile and speak with the same degree of deadly calm that he exhibited.

"I'm very comfortably established, but thank you all the same. Hiram, you were saying—about the four winds?" She gripped the engraved bone-and-bambo piece as if it were a talisman.

Francis shuffled into the room and right back out again without saying a word, and Hiram laboriously got to his feet. "Time for my bedtime pill, m'dear. I'll see you in the morning."

"Hi-ram," Tally wailed.

Thane was practically on top of her by then, and it was impossible to miss the conspiratorial look that passed between the two men. She had been tricked! Even Hume must have had a hand in it—and she had hugged him good-bye, had been so grateful to him for reminding her of Hiram!

"Thane, my contract with you ended at nine o'clock this morning. The specified dates were inclusive. I stayed on until the middle of the afternoon, but don't worry, you won't be billed for overtime. I don't think there's anything more to be said between us." When he didn't reply, but continued to loom over her, boring into her with those intimidating eyes, she gripped the small tile in her hand until her fingers protested. "Well, why don't you go?" she flung out rashly. The next thing, she'd be hanging onto him, watering his shirtfront again, and she didn't think her self-esteem could take another session like that.

He leaned over and covered her fist with a strong, tanned hand, prying open her fingers one by one and removing the mah jong tile. Then he raised her to her feet and she simply sagged there, totally helpless against the strength of his compelling gaze and her own needs.

"Thane . . . what do you want with me?" she implored when the leaden silence had stretched to the breaking point. She was no match for him in a war of nerves, and well he knew it!

"Don't you really know? Even yet?"

She shook her head slowly, unable to trust herself to speak. If he asked her to go on working for him, what could she say? What excuse could she give? She had never been good at dissembling, and the higher the stakes, the more transparent she became. With stakes like these, she'd be blurting out the whole pathetic little story, and he'd have a good laugh over that!

"Thane, why won't you just leave me alone? You know perfectly well I'm not any danger to Hiram, and besides, I'll be clearing out of here tomorrow for good. Or do you want to hang around and frisk me before I go? Is that it?" Her voice was high and strained, and her eyes were clouded with distress. "Well?" she demanded.

"What do you want me to do with the boxes you left behind?" he asked quietly, throwing her completely off-balance.

"Boxes? Oh, those." The last bit of resistance

flowed out of her into the gloomy old parlor and she dropped down onto Hiram's plush-covered loveseat.

Thane followed her down, regaining her hand and searching her averted face. "Tally . . . are you running away from me again? Is that it? Is that why you couldn't wait, even when I specifically asked you to?"

"What do you mean? You didn't ask me to do anything!" Righteous indignation rekindled her resistance and she turned to glare at him accusingly. *He* had been the one to leave without saying goodbye, not she. She wasn't going to allow him to get away with shoving his guilt off onto her shoulders!

"I told Judy to explain that I had a rush call. My operations chief in Orlando was in a wreck this morning and he's in intensive care. I had to go—he has a wife and seven children and they just moved there less than three months ago."

"Oh—I'm so sorry, Thane." And she was. "Is he . . . will he . . . "

"Make it? Yes, I think so. The last report I had was less than an hour ago and he's been moved to a private room. I've arranged for a woman I know to move in and take over the kids so that his wife can spend all her time with him."

"Another job for HouseSpouse," she murmured. "Maybe we should open a branch." She didn't mean to sound facetious—it was purely a nervous reaction —but fortunately, Thane seemed to understand.

"Tally, why are you running?" He was so close she could smell the intoxicating essence of tobacco and sandalwood and healthy masculinity.

"I'm leaving, not running. There's a difference," she said quietly.

"I told you we'd finish our argument once the

battlefield was cleared of unauthorized personnel. Why couldn't you have waited?" His hand moved to cover her twisting fingers.

She jerked her hand away. "Wait for what? For you to . . . to prove that you're physically stronger than I am? That you've got me tied up with a tricky contract and you've discovered a loophole that extends it another week?" She was warming to her subject now, eyes blazing like the sapphire ring she had left on his dresser. "And anyway, the battlefield isn't quite cleared yet, is it? Or maybe Judy's considered authorized personnel!"

"Your stepsister's cleared out, so—"

"She's not my stepsister anymore! Claire's filed for divorce!" Scratch one more marriage from the record. So much for romantic dreams of happy-ever-after!

"I don't give a damn whose sister she is, she can spread herself out somewhere else! I've had it with wall to wall company! I want a—"

"Then what are you griping about? We're all out of your hair now! Go home and wallow in your blasted privacy!"

"Will you shut up and let me finish a sentence?" His nails were white where his fists were clenched—probably in an effort to keep them from around her neck, she thought rancorously.

"Nobody tells me to—"

He shut her up in the most effective way possible. When at last he lifted his head she was completely shattered. Her lips still tingled from the rough caress of his, and the taste of him was on her tongue.

"That's not fair," she mumbled bitterly, drawing away from his arms.

"Probably not, but then, when someone stretched

my patience to the breaking point, I'm afraid my gallantry can't be depended on." He waited, watching like a hawk for her reaction.

"And did I stretch it?" she asked finally, grudgingly.

A gleam shot through his clear eyes and some of the tension seemed to go from him. "You know you did, sweetheart. In every possible way, again and again, and from the first time I laid eyes on you." The air seemed to shimmer between them, and Tally found herself holding her breath. "Tally—tell me what you're thinking, what you're feeling?"

She was feeling a distinct clamminess, as if what little color she had, had drained from her face. Her heart was leaping about like a newly captured bird. "Frightened," she said candidly. And then, "No, more like nervous. Apprehensive."

He looked stricken. "You're frightened of me? God, child, don't you know—"

"No! Not of you." Her eyes clung to his, begging his understanding. She couldn't bear to see him hurt, even over a silly misunderstanding like this. "Thane, never of you . . . At least, not since I realized that you weren't actually going to turn me over to the law for gold-digging." Her smile was tentative, inviting a like response, and she was relieved to see some of the strain leave his face.

"Then why are you nervous?" And then, before she could formulate an answer, he blurted, "Why am *I* nervous? Why are we both sitting here in this museum like a couple of wax figures when all I want in the world right now is to take you to bed and spend all night making love to you?"

Her mouth fell open, and then she closed it, and then her lips parted again as she tried to understand what he was saying.

"Is that your goldfish imitation?" he teased, his eyes almost black as his pupils dilated to cover the irises. One gentle forefinger touched her bottom lip, tracing its fullness and pressing against a tiny pulse that beat there.

"Thane . . . is that really what you want? Is that why you came?" Because if it was—if he wanted an affair with her—then she was willing. She'd take whatever he offered her, for however long. Lord knows, she couldn't suffer any more afterward than she was already. At least she'd have something to dream on after it ended.

"Didn't you know I would?" he asked quietly.

"No— I mean, it never occurred to me— I mean, of course I knew you were . . . well, attracted to me, but—"

"And you, Tally? Are you attracted to me? Would you be willing to come back home with me now?" It was as if he were choosing his words with great care, picking his way carefully through a mine field.

"Yes," she said frankly. "You know I am, Thane."

"How attracted? Enough to cancel your plans to move to Tampa to be with your father?"

"Yes." She was well past any face-saving attempt to lie. And still he seemed to be waiting. "If you want me to . . . to sleep with you, then I will." Why didn't he say something? Had she just made a fool of herself again? "Thane, I don't know how you're supposed to go about these things! You asked me and I answered you, and if that's not plain enough—if you have to have some sort of . . . some sort of a contract—then write it up! I'll sign the blasted thing! I'll do whatever you say, only don't just sit there *smirking* at me!"

"You love me, don't you?" he said softly.

"Of course I love you! What did you think? That I just hop into bed whenever I want to take a load off my feet? Of course I love you, you—you—"

Fortunately, she wasn't given time to come up with the proper epithet. Thane caught her to him and bore her down on the narrow, hard loveseat. His mouth touched lightly on both eyelids, followed the short, narrow course of her nose and came to rest on the target it sought.

"Tally, put your arms around me." His tongue caressed her lips and made a daring foray into the warm cavern of her mouth. Her arms slipped under his rumpled coat and her hands attempted to capture all the wonderful warmth of him, the glowing vitality of his lean, hard muscles. In spite of the cramped position forced on them by the wretchedly misnamed piece of furniture, Thane had managed to align her body in such a way that she was stunningly aware of his readiness.

"Sweetheart, precious, do you have any idea what I'm thinking about right this minute?" he rasped, as his fingers struggled with the fastening of her bra.

"Mmmm, then it's true what they say about great minds?" She pressed herself against him to give him easier access to the hook at her back.

"Darling Tally, do you think you can stand to put up with me for the next fifty years or so? And before you answer, I think I ought to tell you that there's a lot of night work involved. It takes a strong back, too."

"Since when have I ever objected to overtime?" she replied piously. Her hands were tugging the shirt from his belt and meeting with considerable distractions along the way.

"I warn you, I don't believe in short-term contracts. The next one that has both our names on it is the permanent kind—with no loopholes."

"Thane, are you sure?" The cramped, half-playful lovemaking was suspended as he held her face between his hands. It was all there in her eyes for him to see, nor did she try to disguise it. She searched his face for long moments and then a low, anguished sound escaped her as she caught the gleam of tears in his eyes.

"Tally, Tally, don't you know? Couldn't you tell from the very first that I was knocked out of my mind by you? You called it chemistry, my sweet love, and it was that, all right. That, plus a thousand volts of electricity and a hundred other things I've never felt before in my life, including a bad attack of jealousy that almost had me ready to toss up a multimillion-dollar deal just to get that damned puppy, Loggins, out of my house!"

"David! But that was all over even before I saw him again, only I didn't realize it. Darling, by that time, your . . . chemistry had gone to work on me, and after the initial shock of seeing David, there was nothing there except a—a sort of damp splutter. Like wet firecrackers."

"I know. I guess I knew all along, but you were pretty quick to set me straight about the difference between love and chemistry, and I was afraid to move too fast and scare you off. And it seemed like every time I got you in bed, you were in no shape to let me prove anything to you. Remind me to check into the sick leave provisions in our next contract."

"And the maternity benefits," she added.

"Anything else you want stipulated?"

"Contact lenses and a new pair of silver sandals."

His eyes bathed her in a glow of warmth. "I think I can manage that much."

"The accident provision clause. Does that cover breaking both our backs on this blasted instrument of torture?" she groaned as her shoulder encountered a rosewood knob. But instead of replying, he lifted her onto his lap, which brought on another set of delightful perils.

"I'm not sure I can wait until your Dad gets in. Does a bride have to be given away to make things legal, or can someone just take her?"

She lowered her eyes modestly, her hands still busy on his shirt. "Well, I'm sure you can find a few loopholes in my old contract until a better one can be drawn up," she said helpfully, and he stood and lifted her in his arms.

"Then we'd better adjourn to more comfortable quarters. I can see right now we're going to be haggling over the various clauses and stipulations all night."